BUILDERS OF JERUSALEM

BOOKS BY FRIEDA CLARK HYMAN

Jubal and the Prophet
Builders of Jerusalem

BUILDERS OF JERUSALEM

In the Time of Nehemiah

FRIEDA CLARK HYMAN

illustrated by Donald Bolognese

FARRAR, STRAUS & CUDAHY
JEWISH PUBLICATION SOCIETY

Copyright © 1960 by Farrar, Straus & Cudahy, Inc.,
and the Jewish Publication Society of America
Library of Congress catalog card number 60-12281

First Printing, 1960

Published simultaneously in Canada by
Ambassador Books, Ltd., Toronto. Manufactured
in the U. S. A. by H. Wolff, New York

FOR MY MOTHER AND FATHER

Author's Note

Nehemiah shaped the course of Jewish history and, in doing so, shaped the course of world history. Had he not reestablished Israel upon her land, had he not maintained the purity of Judaism, based on the Torah, monotheism—the belief in one God—might have vanished from the hearts and minds of men. That is to say, Judaism would have vanished from the earth, and with the disappearance of the mother religion, Christianity and Mohammedanism would never have emerged.

It took a man of strength and action, as well as a man of vision, to revive the despairing remnant of a people encircled by enemies. Such a man was Nehemiah. He rejected compromises and half measures. If he lost the love of his fellowmen, he counted it a small loss, provided he achieved his purpose and conserved his integrity.

Little is known of Nehemiah's personal life. As far as we know, Nehemiah was unmarried. Some say that he was a eunuch. It is known that certain provinces of the Persian Empire were required to deliver a specified number of eunuchs to the King. But I cannot conceive of a eunuch's wielding such influence on Jewish life. Moreover, to mutilate oneself in any way was and is an abomination to the Jew.

In telling this story, I have had to invent some characters that figure in it—Bani and Oebazus, notably—and have taken some liberties. The issue of Shabbat does not take place until Nehemiah's second visit to Israel, and I have it figure during his first visit, for I believe it must certainly have arisen during the first twelve-year period. Oebazus, although my own invention, figures in no event that might not have happened to many Persians of the time, especially Persian noblemen. The prayer of Artaxerxes is, in history, attributed to Darius. The presentation of the letter in the Temple is related by Josephus. Though much of Josephus regarding Nehemiah is legend, this custom was an accepted one, so the incident as I relate it may be considered factual.

My main sources have been the following: The Books of Nehemiah, Ezra, and Daniel; the Book of Maccabbees, 11; Herodotus; Xenophon; the Jewish Encyclopedia; Josephus' *Antiquities of the Jews;* Graetz' *History of the Jews;* Orlinsky, *Ancient Israel;* Huart, *Ancient Persia and Iranian Civilization;* Abbott, *Darius the Great;* Albright, "The Biblical Period," in *The Jews,* ed. by Finkelstein; Vaux, *Ancient History from the Monuments;* Breasted, *The Conquest of Civilization;* Ceram, *The Secret of the Hittites;* Fox, *Atlas of European History;* Pfeiffer, *Introduction to the Old Testament;* Chubb, *City in the Sand.*

BUILDERS OF JERUSALEM

1

It was dim and close in the classroom. Outdoors there was air, acres of air, and sunshine. Outside too was his friend, Acratheus, who was perhaps swimming or fishing in the Ulai. Bani wished he were with him there, outside, instead of sitting here with the other sons of the Jewish community of Susa. If only the lesson had been concerned with his great heroes, the warrior kings, David or Saul or those mighty men, Jonathan and Joab! But Jeremiah was the subject of that day's lesson. Jeremiah—a prophet who had lived over one hundred years ago. Who cared what he had said!

Master Jadon's voice, soft though it was, reached him in spite of himself. He was asking a question: "And what did Jeremiah prophesy?" The master's long brown beard was streaked with grey; his brown eyes searched each youthful face.

Every hand but Bani's shot up. The boy in front of him spoke. "He prophesied that God would bring us back from that exile."

"And did He?" Jadon persisted.

"Yes," the boy replied, "forty eight years later."

"Then what happened?"

"Twenty-two years after his return to Jerusalem, our holy Temple was rededicated," the same boy went on. "That made seventy years altogether. Exactly as Jeremiah had predicted."

We! Us! Bani said scornfully to himself. What did these boys have to do with such events. They weren't even there. They lived here in Susa, the winter capital of the Kings of Persia. Still, Jadon didn't object to their 'we.' If anything, he agreed.

"And then what happened?" Master Jadon asked. "Did our people remain loyal to God?"

"No," another boy answered. "Fifty-eight years after the Temple was rededicated, Ezra had to leave with more of our people. And he brought us back to God and His Torah."

"So Ezra did," Jadon nodded, "And those who went with him, helped."

Now Bani was all eyes and ears. He stared at his teacher as though hypnotized. Jadon was watching him tenderly. Would he go on? For this, indeed, was what he craved to hear.

"Yes, they were brave and loyal, those followers of Ezra," Jadon said, still looking at Bani, "men and women like Bani's cousins."

The class turned towards him. Instinctively Bani sat up tall. No matter what he felt, he must be upright.

"Why then, Master Jadon," the boy next to Bani blurted out, "didn't you go too? You were Ezra's own student."

Many gasped. Every head had turned back to the teacher. From the corner of his eye, Bani saw a dull red flush color the questioner's face.

It was an insolent challenge. Yet Bani himself had often wondered about this. And not only about Jadon.

"Because Ezra forbade me," Jadon said sadly. It was clear he wasn't angry. "When I pleaded with him, he told me my duty was here in Susa, with boys like you. But someday," and now his voice, full of longing, seemed to come from a great distance, "someday, I hope to follow Ezra, my Master. And perhaps you boys will go too . . ."

Never! Bani shut his lips tightly to keep from shouting the word aloud. Never, never! He wanted no part of that place.

All he wanted was to get out of this classroom. Not that he could meet Acratheus right away. He had to go to the Royal Corridor after school. Nehemiah had commanded him to be there. He wrinkled his nose distastefully. He still had to deliver his uncle's message. Well, he'd have to wait until class was over.

He sat rigidly for the remainder of the morning. Not until all the boys had trooped out did he approach the teacher.

"My uncle would like to know, Master Jadon," he said, standing respectfully before the desk, "if you have any word from . . ." He paused, as if unwilling to pronounce the hateful word, then brought it out: "from Jerusalem."

Jadon examined him searchingly. "And what would you like to know, Bani?"

"I?" startled, his own dark eyes looked into Jadon's. "Nothing," he said, averting his face. "Nothing."

"But you do, Bani."

Then why, he thought bitterly, why didn't Jadon tell him about his parents? Why must he be forced to ask?

"Well, Bani?"

He had to say something. "I, I just wondered why my uncle is so worried."

"About Jerusalem?"

He nodded.

Jadon studied him again, then sighed. "He is right to worry. We Jews, all of us, are worried. There have been reports of attacks by the nations surrounding Judah. And then, of course, there is Ezra . . ." his voice faded. "Do you understand now, Bani?"

"Yes," he bowed, turned quickly, and left the room and the low white house. He understood all too well. But what no one suspected was that he didn't care. Or did Jadon? The possibility dismayed him for the moment. Then he tossed his head. Let him. He was outside at last. And here was Chobi, the groom, with his mare.

In a little while he was at the appointed place in the Royal Corridor. He had left Chobi at the second Great Gate of Susa. Nehemiah, he knew, was still with the King. He had seen Nehemiah's black stallion at the gate guarded by a servant. Chobi had sent the man home.

Bani was not frightened in the Royal Corridor. The Paradise, acres of gardens and hunting grounds, stretched between this Corridor and the Apadana. And in the Apadana, the magnificent hall of audience, sat Artaxerxes, King of Kings. The Apadana, however, still terrified him, although Bani had been presented to the King. The Pylons, towering at the entrance to the Paradise, were like Artaxerxes on his throne: unmoving, remote, powerful. How did his Uncle dare to stand each day before the King? Ah, but Nehemiah was, after all, Nehemiah!

The boy leaned over the parapet. Susa, the beautiful city he loved, lay before him. On the platform below stood the remains of other palaces. Persian kings never lived in the palaces their fathers had built. The lowest platform was dotted with towers—brick fingers raised in warning against all enemies. Down there in the city the Citadel loomed, a city within a city. Fortified and grim, it was kept eternally prepared to receive the King himself, should anyone dare to challenge his rule. As though to seal off this royal part of Susa from its other half, the Ulai canal encircled it, a gleaming serpent.

Bani turned back to watch the strangers who were seeking audience with Artaxerxes. There was an Assyrian with his bronze helmet; and there a Bactrian carrying both javelin and pike; next to him stood a Sacae wearing his pointed cap, and armed with an axe; while on the other side a group of painted Negroes waited. These were Ethiopians of Africa, dangerous, with their long bows and flint-headed javelins.

Persia was a vast Empire, stretching from the Nile Delta to the Aegean Sea, including the entire eastern end of the Mediterranean and from this western boundary eastward, almost to India. She was divided into twenty Satrapies or Provinces, which were subdivided into one hundred and twenty-six districts. Why, a traveller must spend many months to traverse the Empire from end to end! What was that tiny spot called Jerusalem compared to such a domain?

A man ascending the great stairway now drew his attention. Bani wondered from what distant land he had come. He was altogether strange. He carried no peculiar weapon. He was simply dressed in a dark robe and blue turban, without insignia. Or perhaps that red jewel hanging from the middle of his turban was a sign of his national origin.

The newcomer paused on the top of the stairs, looked around the Corridor and to the boy's amazement came directly towards him.

"Is this where one waits for an audience, boy?" He spoke Aramaic, the language of the entire Fertile Crescent.

"Yes, my lord," Bani bowed courteously.

The stranger fixed his ice blue eyes on Bani. The red jewel on his forehead shone above them. "You have been admitted to his Majesty?"

"Yes, I have."

"Today?"

"No." Bani shifted uncomfortably. Who was this man to speak so imperiously to him? He, a son of Hacaliah, was not accustomed to such inquisition. "Two months ago," he said, and angry at himself for answering, he turned unceremoniously away towards the stone parapet.

"A marvellous view." The man remarked, not at all put out. He spoke to Bani from over the boy's shoulders. "What buildings are those, below us?"

"The King's Palace and his Harem." He had no choice but to answer.

"And that mound between them?"

"The Underground fortress."

"And all those towers!" The man did not disguise his awe.

"And our Citadel!" In spite of himself Bani turned around to the west, excited as always by the mere sight of the fortress. How he loved to go there, to practice with the other young boys.

"Our?" the man repeated. "You are a Susian?"

"Of course."

"But you are fair. Susians are dark, almost as dark as Ethiopians."

"Still I am a Susian," said Bani curtly.

"You were born here?"

"No," Bani admitted reluctantly. He had been born in Jerusalem, of course. He was a Jew. He had been only one month old when both his parents had died. A relative had brought him back to Susa, to Nehemiah. Still what business was it of this one? He drew himself up haughtily. "If you will excuse me," he began.

"Bani!" someone called.

The boy turned to the stairway. Oebazus, the Arga-Pat, the Commander of the Citadel, had just come up. Behind him an escort of two soldiers stood stiffly.

The stranger, caught between Bani and the noble-man, scrutinized them for a second, then with a half-bow, moved to the other side of the Corridor.

Oebazus was one of the seven chief advisers to Artaxerxes. He was skilled, not only in soldiery, but in law, as well. His love for law had made him a student of all the judicial systems of the countries of the Persian Empire. It was his interest in the statutes of Torah, that had first brought him and Bani's uncle, Nehemiah, together.

Today the two men, Oebazus, the Persian, and Nehemiah, the Jew, were close friends. Everyone knew that Oebazus' father, a judge before him, had been executed by Artaxerxes for an unjust sentence. But only Nehemiah knew the horror Oebazus had been made to suffer afterwards.

On a seat made of his father's skin, the young Oebazus had been forced to sit and judge.

The day Nehemiah had told this to Bani, the boy had neither eaten nor slept. Of course, this explained why Oebazus had abandoned law for soldiering. Today he was all soldier. Only in exceptional cases was he commanded by the King to sit as judge.

"Greetings, my lord." Bani saluted smartly.

"You have not been at the Citadel lately," Oebazus said. "No more lessons with the lance?"

"But I practise each day. At least an hour."

"Not enough. Why are you so lazy?"

"I must study," he said, then stopped. Oebazus should understand. But from the way the Arga-Pat frowned it was clear he was not satisfied. "I must do what my uncle commands," Bani lamely concluded.

"Your uncle, hmmmm. I must speak to him. Will he raise you to be a man or a scribbler?"

"Both," Bani grinned. "That is, if you speak to him. Otherwise . . ." he let the words fade into their unspoken conclusion.

"What would you rather be, boy?"

"A soldier. One of the King's Guard." Bani said promptly.

"Well spoken." Oebazus' smile was touched with bitterness. He examined the boy carefully. Thirteen, but tall for his age. Bani was wearing a tunic edged with golden embroidery. There were gold bangles on his wrists. His boots were made of the softest yellow leather. "Where is your sword?" Oebazus asked sharply.

Bani raised his shoulders expressively. "At home. I am only allowed to wear it on certain occasions."

Oebazus pressed his lips together, shaking his head in dismay. He gazed over Bani's head at the Pylons. But these offered no help. "I shall have to speak to your uncle," he said. "He must see to your training."

Bani could visualize Nehemiah, and recalled his stern grey eyes. How would he accept such suggestions, even from an Oebazus?

"Tell him to expect me tomorrow evening." Oebazus said. "If he has other plans, ask him to send word."

"Very good." Bani saluted again. The Arga-Pat and his escort disappeared between the Pylons.

It was hot in Susa, even in Kislev. The Susian heaven was, as usual, cloudless. In the distance, dark mountains pierced the skies. Tomorrow he would go with Acratheus, to hunt vultures in those mountains. He already had permission. In fact, his uncle had suggested it.

How he loved Susa! And how proud he was to be a grandson of Hacaliah, a nephew of Nehemiah, Cupbearer of the Great Artaxerxes. Now if only Oebazus could convince his uncle! If he could be done with those lessons each day so that he could be like Acratheus, life would be perfect. Or if, at least, he could learn about the ancestors he really admired: David and his warriors. But to have to sit in a dark room, listening to all that stuff about Jeremiah, or Isaiah or Daniel. Especially Daniel! If Daniel had loved Jerusalem so, why hadn't he gone back there instead of being buried here, right in the middle of Susa?

"Bani!"

He jumped guiltily. But almost instantly he gathered his face together. Of course his uncle could not know what he had been thinking.

"Yes, my lord." He bowed to the man who stood between the Pylons.

"Waiting long?"

"Only this last ten minutes. Besides, Oebazus was here."

"So?" Nehemiah's eyebrows arched above his grey eyes. His hair and beard were carefully curled in the Persian style. The man always seemed so big to Bani, though he was just under six feet. But he was strongly built, with powerful shoulders and chest. His heavy silk court dress was adorned with rosettes, turquoise earrings glinted at each side of his head, a lapis lazuli seal hung from his thick neck, his turban was heavily bordered with gold. Now that he was outside the Apadana, he had fastened a small sword with a jewelled hilt to his belt.

"What did Oebazus have to say?"

"That I should . . ." Bani began, then caught himself. It would never do to repeat every word. "He said he will visit you tomorrow evening, unless you have other plans."

"Good." His uncle crossed the Corridor to the stairway. Bani, joining him, again noticed the stranger. He had drawn his headdress forward so that it covered all of his face but his eyes. Bani shivered. How hard those eyes stared! And were they staring at him, or at Nehemiah, or at someone behind them? Before he could find out the man turned sharply away. But Bani had no time to consider the matter, for they were already descending the stairway.

"Did you ask your teacher whether he had received a message from Jerusalem?" Nehemiah said.

"He has not," he replied quickly, hoping to close the subject. But as the silence grew, he knew how his uncle reacted. Without turning his head, he could see his brows arched, his lips pressed together. It was always so, when Jerusalem was mentioned.

"I see," Nehemiah said at last. "Still, I wonder . . ."

"What, my lord?"

"No, nothing. Well, we shall see. And your lesson," the voice lifted, "how was that today?"

On each side of the stairway a stone lion devoured a stone bull. This was the way he felt, Bani thought. Like that bull, struggling.

"Well, Bani? Have you no tongue? How was your lesson today?"

He would not lie. But how does one say 'awful' to a

■ 12 ■

Nehemiah. "Not good," he muttered, then as they reached the long avenue, the Holiday Pavilion, he burst out: "Why must I study each morning . . . ?" But he did not dare continue.

Nehemiah was black with anger. Bani should have known better. But Oebazus had given him courage. Oebazus, the Susian, no son of Hacaliah.

"You are a Jew," Nehemiah said icily, without breaking his pace.

I am a Susian, Bani wanted to protest, as angrily as he had before that stranger.

As though he had heard his nephew, Nehemiah halted. "Remember, Bani," he added, "if you remember nothing else, that you are a Jew, not a pagan." Then he strode towards the end of the Holiday Pavilion and the Great Gates.

Chobi came forward immediately. He swung the jet black stallion before his Master, and steadied it. Nehemiah mounted with ease. Bani followed on his mare. Once more he was back on the lowest terrace of the Royal City.

The pavements were blocks of limestone resembling marble. The houses gleamed white and blue and green. Here and there bronze doors trapped the sun, glowing like blocks of fire.

A flock of fat-tailed sheep shuffled towards them, probably on their way to the Citadel, but their shepherd herded them to the side, bowing as he did so to Nehemiah. As they turned a corner, a contingent of Sagartians, their lassoes around their shoulders, marched in military formation. Their ranks filled the width of the road.

Nehemiah reined in his horse and waited. The Sagartians advanced. The first rank, eyes forward, threatened to mow down Nehemiah, Bani, and their groom. Nehemiah eyed the soldiers sternly, as they continued to approach. They were only a yard from Nehemiah's mount, when an imperious command rang out.

"Halt!"

The ranks held immediately. An officer, puffing, cut through his men.

"Who dared to give that command?" he demanded.

"I did," said Nehemiah, staring down coldly.

"And who . . ." The officer met Nehemiah's eyes, hesitated, then regained his pluck. "Who presumes to order Sagartians?"

"Nehemiah."

"Oh." The officer reddened. The soldiers behind him were tense. Bani sat up straight. Even the Sagartians knew whom Artaxerxes loved.

"My lord," the officer saluted, "your pardon!" He wheeled about. "Make way," he cried, "make way for Nehemiah, Cupbearer to the King."

Instantly the ranks opened, and their three mounts passed through. Nehemiah rode forward, looking neither to the left nor the right.

At the end of the street, they should have veered to the left, towards home. Instead Nehemiah turned right. Bani's heart swelled with foreboding. He was soon to answer for his recent poor school-work. Sure enough, his uncle stopped before a familiar low white house. He was back at Jadon's.

Chobi dismounted and assisted first Nehemiah, then the boy to dismount.

"Shall I go in, too?" Bani asked, praying for a 'no.'

"Is there any reason for you to avoid your Master?" said Nehemiah, without slackening his pace.

Bani looked unhappily at his uncle's back. What should he say? But the door was already opened. There was nothing to do but follow. Azgad, Jadon's chief disciple, filled the doorway. Without a word, he stepped back and let them pass.

In the room Bani knew so well, twenty Patriarchs of Susa's Jews were studying. The men rose as Nehemiah entered. All except Jadon.

The teacher sat before his table, a parchment unrolled before him. His brown eyes, flecked by the candle's flame, were raised in greeting. Nehemiah approached him. Before the table he bowed. But his anger and arrogance had not vanished. His voice, however, was respectful, as it always was with Jadon.

"Shalom, my Master," he said.

"My son, shalom. Be seated. The class is in session."

"Forgive me, my Master. I cannot stay."

"No?"

"I came for another reason."

Bani held his breath. Now, he would be disgraced. And before all these, the chief men of the community. He would never have believed this of Nehemiah. To shame a son of Hacaliah before others!

"And what is that, my lord?"

"Jerusalem."

A sigh of relief escaped the boy. But he dared not wipe the perspiration from his forehead.

"I told Bani I had no message."

"True, but I wanted to ask the others."

"Is it likely any one of us would have word before Nehemiah?"

"We each have kin who might have arrived. And then," Nehemiah paused, "Ezra was your Master."

"Ah yes, Ezra." The air seemed to stir, as though a soft wind had pierced the stone of the house. Jadon's words were tinged with longing, the same longing Bani had heard that morning. "It is thirteen years since I have seen Ezra," said Jadon, speaking as if more to himself than to the others. "If there were some caravan leaving. . . . Azgad is ready to fill my place here."

"Then no one has heard anything?" Nehemiah addressed the room, recalling Jadon and the others back to Susa. "Not even from one of Ezra's disciples?"

"Not a syllable," Jadon said.

"It is too long," Nehemiah thought aloud. "Unless our enemies have decided to live at peace with us. And even then we should have received some word."

"No news at the Apadana, Nehemiah?" one of the elders asked.

"None I have heard."

"No courier from Jerusalem to the King?" another inquired.

"Not lately. Unless . . ." Nehemiah paused. "Unless," he spoke slowly, "unless I have not been told."

The elders frowned. This could be unpleasant news, serious in fact. If Nehemiah were no longer Artaxerxes' confidant, he might be in disgrace. And Nehemiah was a Jew . . . they were Jews . . .

"Is anything wrong, Nehemiah?" Jadon was the only one who dared to ask.

"No." The Cupbearer said. "No," he repeated emphatically. "Nothing."

The men relaxed. The whims of Kings were too well known to them. None of them was likely to forget Xerxes and Haman. And Xerxes had been the father of Artaxerxes.

"If you hear anything," Nehemiah continued, "you will inform me immediately."

Jadon nodded. Nehemiah bowed, turned to leave, Bani after him. The Patriarchs remained standing.

"My Master," Nehemiah stopped at the door, "Bani wants you to know he will be fully prepared tomorrow."

Jadon's eyes twinkled. "That is good news," he said dryly. And to Bani he added, "At nine o'clock, Bani."

"At nine, my Master." He kept his eyes on his teacher, refusing to read the amusement he knew would be reflected in the faces of the elders.

"Shalom, my lord. Shalom, Bani."

"Shalom," his uncle answered for him. And to the others, he bowed, "Shalom."

The light was blinding after the dimness of the candlelit room. He blinked, smarting with sun and a little shame. But as he cantered between his uncle and Chobi, he had to admit it had not been as bad as it could have been.

Unless, and Bani's hand tightened over the reins, unless there was still a reckoning waiting him at home.

Next day Bani was at Jadon's early. Only three boys had arrived before him. Usually he tiptoed in last, amid the snickers of his classmates.

He had memorized for homework the words of the prophet Amos:

> But let justice well up as waters
> And righteousness as a mighty stream.

When classes were over and as he fairly ran out of Jadon's, his wax tablet bore other verses, from Jeremiah:

> But fear you not, O Jacob, my servant,
> Neither be dismayed, O Israel;
> For lo, I will save you from afar
> And your seed from the land of captivity,
> And Jacob shall again be quiet and at ease
> And none shall make him afraid.

He would have to learn them by heart as well. But he could never take them to heart. *He* was not afraid. *He* was no captive. No one had to save him. Unless it was from such sessions with Jadon. Well, at least Acratheus was waiting for him.

"Here Chobi," he said, as he tossed his tablet and stylus at the groom, and leaped onto his mare. "Let's race."

And before the astonished groom, he spurred his horse homeward. Strangely, no one was about, it was as though Susa had not yet wakened.

In and out of the empty streets Bani galloped until, rounding a bend, a familiar figure appeared, waiting before his gate.

"Acratheus," Bani called out joyfully, waving his hand. Almost a whole day lay before them. And the mountains, the bird hunt . . .

"Bani," the brown-skinned boy cried, and hopped with excitement. "Hurry and come with me."

Bani slid off his mare. "In a minute, after I've eaten."

"No, we can't wait." Acratheus tugged at him. "We'll miss the fun."

"What's your hurry?" laughed Bani. "The vultures will still be there."

"Vultures!" Acratheus' jaw fell. "What are you talking about?"

"You know. We were going to find their nests." He waved towards the mountains. "I even have permission to take a horse for you. Unless," he faltered, "unless you've already found them."

"Oh that." Acratheus' nose puckered disdainfully. "Who cares about that. It's the Makrian I want to see."

"The Makrian? What has the Makrian to do with us?"

"But they're showing him, down at the Gate. The Traitor. You know. The one who rebelled against Persia, against Artaxerxes."

"Oh! That!" Suddenly his stomach tightened with horror. "You mean he's being executed?"

"Of course. But not here. The Makrians will do that themselves. Back in Makran. Here they just cut off his ears and nose."

Bani struggled for self-control. It would never do to let Acratheus know how much he dreaded such a sight.

"But I'd rather go bird-hunting." He tried to make his voice firm. "I want to find the nests."

"Birds! Pooh! What's an old bird compared to this?"

"But, I told my uncle I would go to the mountains." And cunningly, he added, "I have a horse for you for today, Acratheus. Don't you see, I may not be able to get it again."

"You're scared."

"I'm not."

"Yes you are; just like a girl."

Bani gasped. A girl! Those weak useless creatures. One never even saw them. "Don't you dare call me a girl!" he warned.

"Girl! Girl!"

"Here," his fist crashed into his friend's nose, "see if this is a girl's."

They rolled on the ground, punching and kicking. Finally Bani was on top, holding Acratheus' shoulders to the pavement. "Give up?" he asked.

"You're still afraid to see the Makrian."

Bani dug his nails into the other boy's flesh.

"Girl! Girl!"

Bani released him. It was no use. "All right," he said, and got up. "I'll go."

"Good," Acratheus beamed, all anger forgotten, "I knew you would. Let's hurry. Everyone's there already."

"I'll put the mare away."

"Give her to Chobi. Here he comes now."

The groom trotted towards them, his face taut with anger. "How many times must you be told, Master Bani," he demanded without dismounting, "that your Uncle will not have you galloping through the streets! I would be blamed if you were hurt."

"There was no one about, Chobi."

"Because they are at the Gate." And bitterly he added, "To think I have to go with you to the mountains."

"You don't." Acratheus hopped with excitement. "Bani is going to see the Makrian."

"You are?" Chobi stared disbelievingly. "But you Uncle said," he stopped, as one who has caught himself in error, "are you sure, Bani?" he asked curiously, "are you sure you want to go?"

"Sure he's sure." Acratheus cried. "He just told me so. Didn't you Bani?"

"Yes." Bani did not meet Chobi's glance. "What's an old bird anyhow," he muttered.

"Then I'll get a horse for you, Acratheus," Chobi leaped to the ground, delighted. "The Master left orders."

"We'll ride." Acratheus crowed. "We'll be in time."

The next minute the two boys and the groom were cantering towards the First Royal Gate of Susa. Even from the distance they could see the scaffold, an island in a sea of heads.

A roll of drums greeted them.

"Just as I thought." Acratheus stretched to see, from the edge of the crowd. "We didn't have an extra second. See, he's coming now."

A detail of Makrians, Negroes of Asia, marched in military order. Each man's helmet was made of a horse's head, so that he looked part man and part animal. In the center, his hands chained, walked the wretched victim. From his face and both sides of his head, blood streamed.

"His high and mighty lordship," Chobi chortled. "The Governor of Makran."

Bani bent forward over his mare's neck. He dare not disgrace himself. He was faint, and a terrible wave of sourness swept from his stomach to his mouth.

He could not look, but he knew from the sound of the tramping feet, the soldiers and the condemned man were mounting the scaffold.

A flourish of trumpets. The crowd hushed. In spite of his pounding eardrums, Bani heard the announcement.

"Behold the traitor, Shethar, former Governor of Makran. He built the walls of Makran to defy our lord Artaxerxes, King of Kings. He armed the vassals of Artaxerxes against their Master. He spent the taxes of His Majesty for his own treachery."

"Look well, good citizens!" The announcer warned. "See how the King of Kings punishes disloyalty. See and remember."

As though forced by an unseen hand, Bani raised his head. A Makrian soldier had the former Governor by his hair, and was pushing his head up for all to see. Holes, gushing with blood, were all that were left of the victim's nose and ears.

Bani's stomach had a will of its own. All it contained slopped over him, his horse and its trappings.

"Bani." He heard Chobi. "Master Bani."

Bani wheeled his mare and headed back home. Let Acratheus think what he wished, he could have no part in this.

"Master Bani, wait for me."

He urged his mare on. Chobi could remain at the Gate for all he cared. With the rest of Susa.

■ 21 ■

But Chobi's horse was faster. The next moment the groom was in front of him, leading the way. Bani let his reins drop. His mare would follow Chobi, he knew. His head sagged, his chin buried itself in his chest.

He heard his uncle before he saw him.

"Bani! What's wrong?"

In spite of his misery he warmed to the voice. Could it be his uncle was really concerned? "I, I'm all right." He tried to meet Nehemiah's eyes. No, no, he was wrong. His uncle was frowning.

"Where is your friend, Acratheus?" And as neither he nor Chobi replied, Nehemiah continued, "You were supposed to go to the mountains, weren't you?"

"I . . . I went there . . ." Bani waved behind him, southward, "to the Gate, to the Makrian . . ."

"Chobi!"

"Yes, my lord." The groom was pale.

"How dared you?"

"He wanted to go."

"Bani?" Disbelief pierced the boy like a knife. "Impossible!"

"He did, my lord. Ask him."

"Bani . . . ?"

"I, I," Bani tried to speak, but his mouth was dry and as bitter as gall. It was a lie anyhow. He had not wanted to go. Acratheus, Chobi, but not he.

"Well Bani?"

"It was my fault," he cried, "but I did not want to go. I didn't. I didn't." And spurring his mare, he fled up the street to his house, jumped from the saddle, and escaped indoors. Let even Nehemiah think what he would. He hated all people, Persians, Medians, Makrians, . . . But most of all he loathed himself.

2

■ ■ ■ ■
■   ■

A few hours later Bani was summoned to the library. It was a medium-sized room, lined with shelves. Along one wall were ranged a number of huge clay jars sealed with asphalt. In them, Bani knew, were all kinds of business documents. Nehemiah owned land, not only in Susa, but in many of the cities of the province of Elam. Shelves on the other three walls held clay tablets and rolls of parchment. Nehemiah was a lover of books. He employed three scribes just to copy manuscripts. Where, Bani had often wondered, could one more scroll fit. Every inch of space was filled.

A lamp threw its light over the contract Nehemiah was reading.

"Feeling better?" Only the words contained concern. The expression on Nehemiah's face was grim.

Bani nodded. The question he feared was still to come.

"Sit down, then," Nehemiah motioned toward an ebony stool. "Now," he commanded, "explain yourself."

Bani had bathed, changed his garments, been given a cool sweet drink of date juice. He should have been refreshed. But disgust for himself lay in his stomach like an undissolved lump.

"There is no explanation, my lord," he said. "I went. That's all."

"You said you did not want to go."

"I didn't."

Nehemiah's eyes narrowed. "Is it possible my nephew was ordered to go?"

"No." His eyes dropped.

"Then why? Why did you go?" Nehemiah stood over him. "Tell me Bani, how does a son of Hacaliah do what he does not want to do, and what no man can command him to do?"

"Acratheus jeered at me." The words slurred. "He said I was like a girl, afraid to look. He shamed me."

Nehemiah's fist slammed against his desk. "Such," he exclaimed, "is the way of those who do not know God."

The boy dared to lift his head. This was a strange notion. What had God to do with Acratheus? Besides, how could he let Acratheus be blamed for his own cowardice?

"But I'm to blame. I should have said no. I guess," his voice dropped, "I was just a coward."

"Will you be braver the next time?"

"To do what?" Bani was puzzled. Was his uncle disgusted because he had been weak, or because he had joined the crowd?

"To do what your heart tells you is right." Nehemiah shoved a stool close to his nephew. Softly, now he asked, "Do you think, Bani, it is a sign of strength to watch men tortured and disgraced?"

"Then why do they do it?" The boy began to sob, "Why, why?"

"Because they do not understand what our Torah teaches. That man is made in the image of God. If you mutilate man, you mutilate God's image."

"Then why didn't you help him?" Bani clutched at his uncle's sleeve. "You are so close to the King. He would have listened to you."

"Helped him? Whom?"

"The Makrian. Who else?"

"That traitor!"

"But you said . . ." Bani's head swam with confusion. "You just said that man is made in the image of God, well, the Makrian; is he not a man?"

"And a traitor." Nehemiah said harshly. "He deserves death."

"I don't understand," Bani wept, "I don't understand them or you."

"Don't you see Bani, it is because man is touched by God's hand, made in His image, that he must answer for his deeds. The Makrian is a man. He swore allegiance to Artaxerxes. He betrayed his oath. For that he should be, must be punished." Nehemiah paused, then clearly with measured words, he said, "Punished, but not tortured. That is a crime against Heaven."

A rap at the door startled man and boy. "Enter!" Nehemiah called.

A servant bowed from the door. "A visitor, my lord."

"Lord Oebazus?"

"A stranger my lord."

"I am not at home to strangers this evening."

"He said it was urgent."

"I will see him tomorrow."

"He said to tell you it is about Jer-ru . . ." The servant floundered. "There is more to it." He bit his lip, trying to recall, but even as he searched for the other syllables, Nehemiah had shoved him aside and was gone.

"Jerusalem." Bani said to the servant. "It is Jerusalem; nor does it concern you. It does not concern any Susian." Yet even as he spoke he wondered at his own remark. And why was he following the servant after Nehemiah? Why did he suddenly want to hear about that place?

On the threshold of the front hall, Bani stopped. Nehemiah was actually embracing a stranger. "Hanani," the boy heard, "Hanani, my cousin."

Bani examined the man curiously. For an orphan who had never known father and mother, any new relative was important. But what he saw was not impressive. The man was so gaunt, his cheeks were hollows on either side of his nose. His garments were dusty, his sandals worn, and his turban, a vague shade of dirty grey.

"Sit, Hanani," Nehemiah said, "I shall call a servant."

"I am here," Bani said from the doorway. "Can I help?"

"Order a bath, Bani, garments, food."

"Is that all?"

"And come back."

Bani hesitated. "Here?"

"But of course, you must also hear what Hanani has to tell. He comes from Jerusalem."

"Yes, of course," said Bani, and left. "Jerusalem!" That was important. More important than a relative, a cousin.

When he returned, both men were seated. "Come here, Bani," Nehemiah invited, "meet Hanani, your kinsman."

"Welcome, my lord." The boy bowed.

"So this is Bani," Hanani smiled sadly. "This is Reuben's son."

"You knew my father?" Bani bent forward eagerly.

"He was my cousin too, my child. "And," he added, "my best friend."

If only Nehemiah would leave. If only he could speak

to this man alone, and hear about the father he had never known.

"We went together, Bani. He, your mother and I. Together with Ezra."

"Ezra!" To Bani's dismay, Nehemiah interrupted. "How is he, Hanani?"

"Like Jerusalem, Nehemiah. Helpless."

Nehemiah turned pale. "Surely I did not hear you," he whispered.

"You did, Nehemiah." Hanani said sadly. "Ezra is old, too old to control our people. And the city," Hanani shook his head, "she is profaned. Her walls are broken, her gates burned by our enemies. In a little while she will be deserted."

"No!" Nehemiah had risen. "No, it can't be that bad. It mustn't be."

"But it is, Nehemiah."

"But why? Are our enemies that much stronger? What has happened?"

"What we deserve." Hanani sank back against his chair. "God has given us a chance to come home, and we have rejected it." He stopped, bit his lip. "I am sorry, Nehemiah. I did not mean to reproach anyone, but time is running out . . . I have come here for help."

Nehemiah buried his head in his arms. Never had Bani seen Nehemiah so stricken. Nehemiah, who was stronger than any man. The silence grew more and more oppressive.

Finally his uncle raised his head. "You must not reproach yourself, Hanani," he said. "You had to speak. The blame is ours."

"You will help me then to recruit new men."

"More than that, Hanani!"

"More?"

"I shall go myself."

"You!" Hanani sat upright. "But you cannot. You are Cupbearer to the king."

The oil wick sputtered, as though in warning. "I know," Nehemiah said, "but I shall go . . . somehow."

"Nehemiah!" Hanani was out of his chair. Spent as he was, he had seized his cousin's broad shoulders with new-born strength. "Don't do it. Stay here. You will help us more by remaining near Artaxerxes. We have so many enemies in Israel. Sanballat, for example."

"That Samaritan?"

"Yes. He, and all the Samaritans want rights in our Temple. But there are others, just as dangerous. Arabia is afraid we are becoming her trade rival." He laughed bitterly. "And so many of our people have no bread in Judah . . ."

"No bread either!" Nehemiah clenched his hands at his sides. "Then there is no question of where I belong."

"But these men, Nehemiah. They send lies to Susa. For all we know one of them might be at Court this very moment. You must be at Court too, to answer for us, you must be our spokesman."

"No," Nehemiah said. "You told the truth the first time. We have been given a chance. I and all Jews have been given a chance. I must return."

"Where to, Nehemiah?"

Three heads turned. Oebazus stood before them. His eyes roved from Nehemiah to Hanani.

"You expected me, my friend, did you not?"

"Oebazus!" With an almost visible effort, Nehemiah returned to Susa.

"I did not let the servant announce me. But if I am intruding . . ."

"No, no, you could never intrude." Nehemiah had recovered. "Come Oebazus, meet my cousin, Hanani of the house of Hacaliah."

"Your cousin?"

"He has just arrived from Jerusalem."

"Oh." Then bowing he said, "Welcome, my lord. And what is the news from Jerusalem?"

"Bad, Oebazus," Nehemiah answered for Hanani. "Very bad."

"That bad?" Oebazus searched their faces.

"So bad, I must go there."

Oebazus stared, disbelief sharpening the pupils of his eyes. "You cannot mean that," he said at last.

"That is what I tried to tell him," Hanani said. "You tell him, my lord. Tell him he must not go."

"Must not! He cannot!" Oebazus exclaimed. "The Cup-bearer of Artaxerxes does not leave when the desire strikes him."

"I shall ask permission."

"You will do what?"

"I shall ask the King for a leave of absence."

"You would dare ask such a thing, Nehemiah? Do you know what you are saying?"

"Still, I shall ask it."

"Just like that!" Oebazus was hoarse with anger. "And Artaxerxes, what will he say? Run along like a good boy? And he will never suspect you of disloyalty? He will say it is perfectly natural for Nehemiah to want to leave? After all, being Cupbearer to the King isn't a very honorable position. Nehemiah should strive for a more important office, such as Prime Minister, or Regent . . ."

"I shall return to Jerusalem, Oebazus," Nehemiah said calmly.

"Madness!" Oebazus pounded a fist against his open palm. "Madness!"

"Then of what danger to Persia would I be in Jerusalem?"

"That's just it. No one in his right mind would believe you would give up such a position for a post in that insignificant land. They would believe you were leaving Susa to plot. . . . Certainly it would give Artaxerxes pause . . . and for a King to think . . . to suspect . . ." The voice of the Arga-Pat fell . . .

"What do you yourself think, Oebazus?" Nehemiah asked sternly.

"I?" Oebazus was startled. "But what do I matter?"

"Tell me, Oebazus. Why do you think I want to go to Jerusalem?"

Oebazus' jaw dropped. Slowly he shook his head. "Since you ask, I don't think I do or could understand."

"But you would not think me capable of treason, Oebazus?"

"Nehemiah!"

"What is wrong, Oebazus?"

"I know you, Nehemiah."

"And does not Artaxerxes?"

"Artaxerxes' father was assassinated by his own chamberlain. His own brother was accused. Falsely. Artaxerxes slew that older brother. That is why he is king today."

Nehemiah's shoulders sagged. "Still I must go. How I shall ask, I don't know, but the God of my fathers, the God who saved Daniel from the lions, shall be with me to put the proper words in my mouth."

For a heartbeat Oebazus was silent. Then carefully he said, "Your God is a different God, Nehemiah. Had I not read the laws of His Torah, I would still know He is unique. For you and your brothers have clung to Him in defeat, in exile. But Artaxerxes is our master here. He can do whatever he pleases . . . and does. . . ."

"Artaxerxes is the servant of God. No," Nehemiah would not let his friend interrupt him, "not of Ormazd nor Ahriman, the gods of the Persians, but of our God, the God of all Heaven and earth. He will do what God desires."

Oebazus bowed. "May your God protect you, Nehemiah. You will need His help. I know." Softly, now, Oebazus added, "If you are really determined on it, my lord, let the boy stay with me."

"The boy!" Nehemiah's eyes turned quickly toward his nephew. Bani had backed into a corner of the room. "Leave Bani? But why?"

"He will be safe with me. I'll train him to take his place as a Guardsman in the Immortals. He is entitled to his rank with the sons of other noblemen."

"But Bani must go with me."

"To Jerusalem!"

"Who has a better right? He was born there."

"Bani! But I have known him since he was a baby."

"He was brought back to me when he was an infant. My brother, his father, is buried there. So too is his mother. He will be returning home. Shall you not, Bani?"

No, he wanted to protest, wanted to say, I am a Susian, I would rather stay here, become a Guardsman. . . . But one did not say no to Nehemiah. One only nodded one's head obediently.

"Yes, my lord," he whispered.

"It is your bedtime now, Bani."

"Yes," he started for the door.

"Good night, Bani," Oebazus said.

"Good night," he replied.

"Good night," Hanani called after him.

But Bani pretended not to hear. He did not want to speak to this stranger, cousin or no cousin. It was he who had started all this. He and his Jerusalem.

But even as he lay upon his bed he could not help wondering about that mysterious city. What secrets did it contain that it could have drawn his unknown parents there, could make Nehemiah risk his life for its sake?

He clenched his fists beneath the covers. Soon, too soon, he might know. Unless, and in the dark he cowered, unless Oebazus spoke truly.

If Artaxerxes were to suspect his Cupbearer!

The recollection of the bloody head of the Makrian froze the tears that sprang to his eyes.

3

For the next two days Bani moved as in a mist. He knew, as did all Susa, that Nehemiah, Cupbearer of the King, was not at Court.

Had Hanani not come, no Jew would have been concerned. Court officials were sometimes absent and for many reasons, illness, for example. In fact no man dared appear before the King of Kings in anything but the best of spirits and health.

With the other Jews in Susa, Bani waited. Nehemiah never left the library. Nor did anyone enter it.

The morning of the third day, Bani woke more terrified then ever. Some sixth sense warned him this was the day. Yet he could turn to no one. The very walls and halls of the house were distant, threatening. So cut off was the boy, he would have welcomed even a Hanani.

He tried to eat his breakfast, but terror increased with each mouthful. What should he do? He could not go to Jadon, any more than he had gone these last two mornings.

Perhaps he should seek out Acratheus? At least he could speak to him, explain his fears. . . .

Explain what? Speak of whom? Nehemiah? No more than he could speak of those parents lying in Jerusalem's soil.

Suddenly he heard footsteps. He rose, trying to control his trembling. It must be his uncle. After all, he had to leave for the Apadana some time.

The door opened. He half rose, and gasped with amazement. Before him stood Jadon. It took him a second to gather his wits.

"Shalom," he tried to say, but his voice broke.

Jadon approached him, slowly and purposefully, with no return of greeting to soften his advance.

"My master," the boy said, with a bow, surprised at his own surge of joy. He should have feared this man. He had not been at classes these last two days. But instead, he was grateful for his presence, for the help he would give him. For he had no doubt Jadon would know what to do.

"Bani," Jadon pushed him down into his chair, "sit quietly and listen. This is serious."

The boy frowned. He didn't have to be reminded.

"Bani, your uncle must not leave Susa."

The boy stared. Motionless, he waited . . .

"Do you understand, Bani? Nehemiah must remain here."

Bani tried to speak, but his mouth was as dry as sand.

"If he even asks Artaxerxes, he may put every Jew of Persia in peril."

The boy summoned all his control. "Hanani," he whispered, "Hanani is to blame."

"No. Hanani knows better than all of us how important Nehemiah is at the Court. Hanani has been with me since he left your house." Jadon's voice dropped. "He is crushed with fear. For Jerusalem, and for all of us here."

"What can I do?" Bani asked. "You, perhaps, my Master, you are the only one he might obey."

"Obey," Jadon half-smiled, "that is not in Nehemiah's vocabulary."

"He respects you, my Master."

"He loves you, Bani."

"Me!" A bitter cry tore from his throat. "Not me. He loves only," he caught himself. Jerusalem, he had almost said.

"Only what, Bani. Say it!" And as Bani remained silent, Jadon took him by the shoulder. "This is no time for deceit. Your uncle, your people, your land may be in danger."

"There is nothing I can do," Bani said sullenly.

Jadon released him. "You are wrong, child," he said gently. "You are the only one who has any power. If you speak to your uncle, beg him to remain, he might listen . . ."

"Never," Bani shook his head. "Besides, what could I say?"

"That you love him. That because of your love you need him. That without him you have no one."

He tried to imagine such words on his lips. "No," he said, "no, I couldn't."

"*Don't* you love him, Bani?"

"I," the boy faltered, "I don't know."

"Don't you?" Jadon smiled sadly. "Then imagine him denounced by the King as a conspirator, a traitor."

A vision of the Makrian rose before him. "No!" His hands covered his eyes.

"Then go to Nehemiah."

He got up stiffly. He didn't even look at Jadon. His feet with a will of their own carried him out of the room and down the hall to the library. Without knocking he turned the knob and entered. The closed shutters kept most of the sun's rays out. The room, as far as he could see, was empty. But no, someone was there, weeping. Then from the corner, he heard it, through a veil of tears.

"I beseech You, O Lord, the God of Heaven, the great and awful God, who keeps covenant and mercy with them that love Him and keep His commandments . . ."

There was someone on the floor, rocking back and forth, as from the depths of pain. He tiptoed over, afraid to see, yet unable not to see.

". . . and let Your ear now be attentive, and Your eyes open, that You may hear the prayer of Your servant, which I pray before You at this time, day and night for the children of Israel who have sinned against You."

It was a voice he barely recognized. Bani peered closely, as the words continued to pour into the shadows of the room.

". . . yes, I and my father's house have sinned. We have dealt very corruptly against You, and have not kept the commandments which You did command Your servant, Moses. Unto him, you said; if you deal treacherously, I will scatter you abroad among the peoples, but if you return unto Me and keep My commandments, though you were scattered in the uttermost part of the Heaven, yet will I gather them from there and will bring them unto the place that I have chosen to cause My Name to dwell therein. . . ."

It was Nehemiah! But neither the tongue nor the costume belonged to him. He had no shoes on; ashes covered his head, and shoulders. Nothing marked him as Cupbearer to the King. Not even his seal, his constant companion, hung from his neck.

"O Lord I beseech You, let now Your ear be attentive to the prayer of Your servant. . . ."

Should he leave? For surely this was no one he knew. Neither his uncle nor the Court Official. No Sagartians would break ranks for this heap of flesh.

". . . and prosper, I pray You, Your servant this day, and grant him mercy in the sight of the man, Artaxerxes."

Bani was half-way out of the room. He could never talk to this stranger behind him.

"Bani!"

He halted. Had he heard correctly?

"Bani? Is that you?"

He turned swiftly now. Nehemiah was standing, watching him.

"My lord," a knife of sunlight that cut through the blinds lay across Nehemiah. The beard was matted, the cheeks shrunken. Almost, he resembled Hanani.

"Who sent for you?"

"I, I had to find you." It was not difficult to speak after all, for at least he could recognize this sternness.

"And now that you have found me?"

This was his opportunity. He must tell Nehemiah of his fears, his needs, his love . . . without his uncle, Bani had no one . . . Jadon's words flashed through his mind, but he dared not utter them. Despite ashes and bare feet, Nehemiah was still Nehemiah.

"I am relieved, my lord."

Did those grey eyes actually twinkle? No, he must be imagining it. The question was as curt as ever. "Who sent you, Bani?"

It should have been easy to say 'Jadon.' But he could not. Was it because it was only partly true?

"Well, Bani?"

"The Makrian." The name spoke itself. It flashed like a signal, and all his terror responded.

"The Makrian! What are you talking about, boy?"

"Do not speak to Artaxerxes," Bani implored. "He will accuse you of a plot against him. Oebazus warned you. Even Hanani. Don't, my uncle! He will do to you what he did to . . . to the Makrian."

"Bani, here . . . hush lad."

"No, you must not. Please. . . ."

"There is nothing to fear, Bani. I have taken all precautions."

"You have?" The boy gasped. "But how, where?"

"From here, in this room."

"But no one has entered this room, not even the servants."

"Servants are of no help. Nor, for that matter, are masters. Except One, our Master in Heaven, Bani."

"Oh."

"Have you no faith at all, Bani?"

He wanted to say yes, but he could not. Besides, God had taken his parents. And they had lived in Jerusalem, the one city He was supposed to love above all. Or so at least, Jadon maintained. Even his uncle said that; '. . . the place that I have chosen to cause My Name to dwell therein . . .' What would prevent Him from taking Nehemiah?

"What troubles you, Bani?"

"How can we be sure He hears, my lord?"

"He hears all who call upon Him. He heard Daniel in a den of lions. Perhaps I shall be worthy. . . ."

"And if He doesn't?"

"Whatever the result, Bani, for Israel's sake I dare not be silent."

The boy hung his head. It was always the same. Israel's

sake. Jerusalem's. Zion's. Judah's. Call it by any name—
that was all that mattered to Nehemiah.

"Don't you agree, Bani?"

Perhaps because he was so hurt he refused to be convinced. Or perhaps the dimness of the room, concealing
most of his uncle, gave him courage.

"No," he replied. "I do not. Susa means more to me
than Israel."

"Bani!" he saw the hand raised.

"You asked me." He did not flinch.

Slowly the hand dropped. "Then you do not want to go
with me?"

How sure Nehemiah was of being permitted to go!
"No," said Bani.

His uncle was at the window now, opening the blinds.
The sun flooded in, chasing the shadows.

Nehemiah seemed to lean against the sunlight. Then,
as though he had gathered strength from its rays, he faced
his nephew. "You are sure you want to remain in Susa?"

It was harder in the full light of day. Still his answer
was clear. "Yes."

His uncle inspected him, as though he were seeing him
for the first time. The silence was almost more than he
could bear. Finally Nehemiah said, "I shall be leaving for
the Apadana in an hour. After I have bathed and dressed.
Be ready to go with me. In Court dress."

He started. Without thinking, he asked, "The King has
granted me an audience again?"

"No, but he will."

"How can you tell?"

He saw the anger on his uncle's face, and its immediate
suppression. "He will call you," Nehemiah said coldly,
"and you," the pronoun rang with contempt, "you shall
have your desire. You shall remain in Susa."

That 'you' burned in his ears. As he washed and dressed, he could still hear it.

Not even the hooves of his mare or of the stallions of Nehemiah and Chobi could muffle the sound of contempt.

At the second of the Great Gates, he dismounted, leaving his mare with Chobi. With Nehemiah, he went through the Holiday Pavilion, up the Great Stairway, to the Corridor. He would have stayed at his usual post, but Nehemiah waved him on. Between the Pylons, through the Paradise, and out upon the sun-bricked terrace before the Apadana.

"Wait here," Nehemiah commanded.

As Bani watched, the carved doors opened for the Cupbearer of Artaxerxes.

But Nehemiah did not immediately enter. Instead, he turned to Bani and paused, as though he expected a sign from the boy. As Bani did nothing, Nehemiah turned upon his heels and disappeared.

Bani paced the terrace. Susa lay below him. But he could not see it. His own despair crowded out palaces, towers, Citadel.

Yet he had spoken the simple truth. He did want to remain in Susa.

Was that such a terrible admission? Even Nehemiah lived in Susa, had lived here all his life. He had waited for a Hanani to remind him of his duty towards Jerusalem. His father and mother had not waited. For a moment he was proud of his unknown parents.

Then a slow anger began to seethe within him. He walked up and down the terrace, aware of nothing but his own thoughts. Let Nehemiah be as furious as he liked. Let him think what he liked. He was no hyprocrite. If the price of truth was contempt, he'd accept it.

He paced fast now, his feet keeping step with his rage. Stay in Susa he would. Nehemiah had assured him of that. Well, good! He'd live with Oebazus. Right at the Citadel. And someday, by Ormazd, he'd be a soldier.

There'd be no more Jadons, either. No more Amoses or Jeremiahs or Daniels. No more Jerusalems.

He could imagine himself as part of the noble corps, a guardsman. He would have a lance adorned with a golden pomegranate. He would be so brave that he would be appointed to protect the King's very person. Men would respect him and fear him. Bani ben Reuben of the house of Hacaliah would one day be as famous a name as Nehemiah. They would hear of him across rivers and deserts, even in far off Jerusalem. Or better still, he'd arrive in Jerusalem someday as the King's Emissary. They would see what it meant to be a general of Persia. He could imagine the troops drawn up at attention. Oh, the fear he would carve on each soldier's face as he walked up and down their ranks! Then Nehemiah would come to meet him, carefully, warily, and with reverence . . . and before his uncle could bow to him, he would bow first, kiss Nehemiah's hand, would forgive him. It would be sweet to see how grateful Nehemiah would be. . . .

"My lord."

He started. He hadn't heard the soldier approaching. "Yes."

"The King commands your presence."

The King! His dream of the future vanished before the reality of the present. Nehemiah was with the king. He had done what he had said he'd do. He had secured him an audience. But what of Nehemiah's own plans? Had he asked the King permission to leave? And what had Artaxerxes said?

"This way."

He followed meekly, as the soldier preceded him. Could the soldier hear the thump thump thump of his heart? For his uncle was surely under arrest, sentenced. . . . Already, perhaps in chains.

He could barely see the Apadana opening for him. The colored stones beneath his feet blurred into each other. The sentinels at each door might have been stone. Glazed tiles mounted the curved stairway with him. But he saw none of their details. Neither griffin nor lion, neither King nor fire-altar.

At the doorway of the Throne Room, the soldier halted. Ahead of Bani stretched an expanse of wood and marble. Columns, a forest of them, glittering with jewels and brilliant colors, marched along the side of the vast room. And at the farthest end, facing him, seated on his raised throne, was the King of Kings, Artaxerxes the First. There was someone below him, and to his left, but Bani had eyes for no one but the one he sought, Nehemiah. Where was he? Dear God, where was he?

"Bani, the son of Reuben of the house of Hacaliah!" His name rang out like a trumpet's blast.

Dumbly he advanced down the length of that neverending hall. His eyes, like two frightened birds, darted to right and left, but he dared not turn his head.

At the foot of the throne, he knelt.

"You may approach."

He climbed the steps and knelt again, kissing the golden scepter extended to him. A wave of perfume swept down over him. Damasia, Chief Wife of the Harem must also be present.

"Rise, Bani, son of Reuben."

He stood face to face with Artaxerxes himself. Shrewd eyes studied him. A thick beard, curled and rolled, covered most of the King's chest. Instead of a crown, he wore his *cidaris,* a tiara, widening towards the top. His robe was candys purple in hue, of Median origin, with precious stones woven into its fabric, and covering his whole body down to his feet.

On a lesser throne, Damasia reclined. Kohl darkened her eyes and lashes, and rouge stained her full lips. It seemed to the boy that she smiled at him.

Two Guardsmen, each armed with an axe, hovered, over the royal couple, without taking their eyes off Bani.

"You have grown, Bani," Artaxerxes said.

"Yes, Your Majesty."

"You will be a fine man."

"I hope so, Your Majesty."

"A fine soldier."

"If it please Your Majesty."

"And will that not please you?"

"To serve Your Majesty will please me."

The royal eyes twinkled. Aside he said, "The boy is already a courtier. He will do well at the Apadana."

"I pray that it may be so, Your Majesty," said another voice.

Bani's heart leaped. Nehemiah had spoken. Then, he was not a prisoner!

"Your uncle offers you as hostage, Bani. Do you agree to it?"

"Hostage!" Bani was startled. What did that mean? If only Nehemiah, or someone, would speak. "I am afraid, Your Majesty, that I don't understand," he faltered.

"Didn't your uncle explain?" Artaxerxes watched him closely.

His fear grew. This was delicate ground. Carefully he said, "Not about being a hostage, Your Majesty."

"Why not, my lord Nehemiah?"

Bani was grateful that court etiquette forbade his turning from the King. Otherwise he might have had to face his uncle.

"It is not necessary for him to know everything, Your Majesty."

"But what if he wanted to accompany you?"

"He doesn't."

It was a flat statement. Nehemiah was too proud to disgrace a son of his household before others. But Bani was not fooled.

"Your uncle wishes to return to the land of his fathers, Bani," Artaxerxes announced. "Because of my great love for him, I have granted his request, and have appointed him to be the new Governor of Jerusalem."

Nehemiah was safe! Bani's eyes stung with tears, as if pricked with needles. Tears of relief.

"But I want him to come back," the King continued, "he is too precious to lose forever."

"I shall always be Your Majesty's loyal servant," Nehemiah said.

As though Nehemiah had not spoken, the King went on, addressing Bani, "To guarantee his return, he has offered you, his dearest kinsman, to remain here as hostage."

Bani struggled to control his tears. His dearest kinsmen. Was that how Nehemiah had described him?

"Well Bani, what do you say? Would you be content here at Court?"

His moment had come. He had but to say 'yes' and it would turn out as he had hoped. Nehemiah safe. He with Oebazus, a future Guardsman in Susa.

"If it is the King's desire," to his own amazement, his tongue was speaking of its own accord, "then of course, I shall be content. But," and now it was no longer an uncontrolled tongue; his own mind was shaping each syllable, "but if Your Majesty please, I would go to Jerusa-lem."

Had someone started? Or was he straining for a sound?

"Why, Bani?" Artaxerxes' eyes narrowed uncomforta-bly.

"Because, because," his mind sought frantically for the right reply. Ah, this was it. "It is the land of my fathers too," he said firmly. "My parents are buried in Jerusalem."

The King nodded; sadly, the boy thought. "You are Nehemiah's nephew," Artaxerxes said, "these were almost his words. 'The place of my fathers' graves' is what your uncle said." The King lapsed into a dreamy silence. No one dared speak. Finally Artaxerxes, himself, broke that silence. "There are no deeper roots," he murmured. "Fathers, sons. . . ." Then, crisply, as though waking, he commanded, "My Lord Nehemiah," he raised his scepter, "my lord Cupbearer, approach."

From behind him, Bani heard his uncle ascending. Now he was at his side.

"My lord, set me a time for your return."

"May the King live," Nehemiah said, "let it be set at fifteen years."

"Fifteen! No!"

"Fourteen, Your Majesty?"

"Why so many, Nehemiah?"

"Jerusalem is not any city, Your Majesty. It is God's holy Mountain. But if it seem too long for the King, let him set me twelve years. I am sure I shall need at least twelve."

The King sighed. "Let it be." He paused. "How shall I help, Nehemiah?"

"If it please the King, let letters be given to me to the governors beyond the River Euphrates, that they may let me pass through till I come unto Judah."

"Granted, my lord. What else?"

"And another letter to Asaph, the keeper of the King's parks near Jerusalem, that he may give me timber to make beams for the gates of the Citadel of Jerusalem, which belongs to the Temple, and for the wall for the city and for the house where I shall reside."

"You have planned well and carefully, Nehemiah."

"This is the labor of the Lord, Your Majesty."

"Then may your God remember me and my house, for my well-doing."

"I shall lay your letter before Him, Your Majesty."

Artaxerxes extended his hand. "Go in peace, Nehemiah."

Nehemiah knelt and kissed the royal hand.

"Arise my lord Cupbearer." And as Nehemiah stood, the King, to Bani's amazement arose from his throne, Damasia at once rising to her feet, likewise. "Twelve years are a long time, my lord," Artaxerxes said, and his eyes stared off as into a distance. "Why do I let you go? At least why do I not keep Bani against your return?"

Bani's eyes blurred with fear. Was the King about to go back on his word?

Artaxerxes' sight focussed upon the boy. "Can you tell me why, Bani?"

"I think so, Your Majesty," he managed to whisper.

"Why then?"

"My uncle's word is his hostage."

The King was silent. Bani clamped his teeth to hold back his despair. He had probably undone all, with his boldness.

"Yes," the King was speaking. For the second the boy could barely make out that word. "Of course," he heard him now. "That is it exactly. I have accepted his word above the words of those others." Suddenly the royal eyes squinted unpleasantly. "It would not go well with him who deceived me. No matter how much I loved him."

Icy fingers clutched at Bani's heart. The Makrian's disfigured head rose up before him. But Bani stood straight, and stared hard at a point above the King's head.

Artaxerxes raised his scepter. A trumpet blew. Nehemiah and Bani stepped aside. The King and Damasia descended the stairs. The two Guardsmen, their axes ready, marched directly behind them.

It was then Bani noticed the longer right hand of Artaxerxes. The King was deformed; crippled; and the mightiest man in all the world.

The royal couple had reached the door. Suddenly the King turned. Bani and Nehemiah bowed.

"Farewell, Nehemiah," Artaxerxes called. "Farewell, Bani. Love me as you love Jerusalem."

Bani's eyes dropped. He hardly breathed. If the King but knew. He loved that city no more than he had this morning. But he could never have remained here without Nehemiah. This much he did know.

4

Bani woke next morning to a different house. His room was the same: stool, basin, couch, in their usual places. But sound was clearer; footsteps more purposeful.

He peered into the hall. A servant carrying linens moved as though he were a priest offering sacrifice. From his window he saw Chobi heading for the stables, head down, absorbed.

Before he was fully dressed, he was called to the library. The room, always so serene, was topsy turvy. Most of the jars, containing contracts and deeds, were unsealed. Two secretaries were busy with quill and parchment.

As for the manuscripts, almost half were gone. The once cluttered shelves were now comfortable with scrolls. What had happened to them, Bani wondered? More than any other possession, he knew, his uncle prized his books.

"Good morning," Nehemiah greeted him.

"Good morning."

"I have been making plans for the journey, Bani; and arrangements for you," Nehemiah said.

"To help in the library?"

"No," Nehemiah said, "you have more important business."

"Master Jadon . . . ?"

"No, Master Jadon is not able to help you this time. I have arranged for you to live at the Citadel."

"The Citadel!" Bani paled. Could it be he'd have to remain in Susa after all?

"But you wanted to be a soldier, a Guardsman," Nehemiah studied him curiously.

"But the King," the boy stammered, "the King said I can go. . . ."

"And so you shall," Nehemiah said evenly. "But we are going on a long," he paused, "a dangerous journey, perhaps. You must take your place in the ranks with the other young soldiers."

"We are to have an army?" Bani was awed.

"An escort, really."

"But Master Jadon said Ezra refused protection when *he* went up to Jerusalem."

"The King has commanded it. I must consider my rank; his Cupbearer travels with an escort."

"Cavalry, my lord? Infantry?" Bani almost sang out the questions.

"Cavalry, and you must not be found wanting, either with the lance or the arrow."

"Oh, I shall not be," Bani cried. "I shall be the best soldier. I can already use the lance and Oebazus says. . . ."

"Yes, I know," Nehemiah imterrupted dryly, "Oebazus praises his pupil. I would that Master Jadon could do the same."

Bani flushed. It was all too true. But at least he was

through with lessons. He'd be a soldier after all, a real one, like David, Joab . . . With arrows, rations, campfires. Ha, what would Acratheus say to that?

"You may go now. You are expected at the Citadel."

Why did his uncle smile so oddly? Was it so amusing that he, Bani, was to be a soldier? Well, he'd show him.

"And Bani," Nehemiah continued, "this is no game. This is real soldiering. Remember, you're a son of Hacaliah!"

"Of course, my lord," Bani replied stiffly.

"We leave in four months. You shall return only for Shabbat. Other than that, we shall not see each other." Nehemiah inclined his head. "Shalom."

"Shalom." Bani bowed and walked with measured steps from his uncle's presence. But once on the other side of the door he could not contain himself. No more tablets, no more stylus, no more lectures on prophets, on laws. . . . He was free. He could hardly wait to shout the good news. But to whom? Ah, yes. He ran out to the stables.

"Chobi! Chobi! Guess what?"

The groom's apron was streaked with oil. He lifted the rag from the saddle he was polishing.

"What is it, Master Bani?"

"I am to be a soldier."

"And I the Arga-Pat." The groom bent to the saddle.

"But it's true. I am."

"And who said that?"

"Nehemiah."

"He did?" Chobi's lips were pursed. "And all the time I thought it was Master Jadon."

"Stop it!" Bani stamped his foot. "Can't you see it's true? I'm leaving for the Citadel at once."

Chobi eyed him silently. "Really, Bani? On your honor?"

"I don't blame you for not believing. I could hardly believe it myself. But it is true. I'm going now. And if you see Acratheus," his voice lifted, "tell him I can't waste any more time fishing or hunting. I'll be too busy with men. With soldiers."

"Very good, Master Bani." Chobi turned aside to hide his smile. "And now, I suppose you'll be wanting your mare." He led the horse from its stall, fixing a saddle on its back. "I'll be with you as soon as I get out of this apron."

"You? What for?"

"To take you the the Citadel. What else?"

"But I don't need you any more. I'm a soldier now. I can go by myself."

"To be sure," Chobi agreed. "But I shall go with you nevertheless. Those are my orders."

"Those *were* your orders. But I'm a man now. My uncle said so." He mounted the mare. "Farewell, Chobi. Until Shabbat."

Before the groom could stop him, he had the horse out of the stable, and was cantering in a northeasterly direction, toward the Citadel. He heard his name being called but refused to look back or wait.

The Citadel was a semi-circular structure walled in by polished stones. Just outside its walls was the Tomb of Daniel—a spot sacred to Jews and Persians alike. The Ulai flowed nearby. Many Susians claimed that evil travellers sailing past the Tomb were swallowed by the canal's waters.

On this joyous day Bani would have preferred not to be reminded of Daniel. Yet as he passed the arched entrance of the Tomb and the enormous poplar shading its approach he could not help thinking upon this Jew, his ancestor. Nehemiah spoke so often of him. Had Daniel been like his uncle? Daniel had braved the lions of the jungle. Nehemiah was about to brave dangers as great, and, like Daniel, without weapons. Unless, perhaps, faith was a weapon?

"Halt!"

He reined in his mount. So lost in thought had he been, he had forgotten where he was going.

"Who goes?" The soldier's pike pointed at him.

"Bani of the house of Hacaliah."

The pike was instantly vertical. The soldier struck it upon the ground. "Enter!"

Bani passed between two bronze gates. The fortress lay before him.

The castle of the Citadel occupied but a fraction of its space. For acres about, there was nothing but grassless and trampled fields. Wherever one looked, there were soldiers, troops of every kind, mounted and afoot. Everywhere the sun glanced off lances, swords, shields, slings, bows, arrows, chariots.

Bani's whole body throbbed with anticipation. Where would he be put? He could see himself dashing across the plain, charging the enemy.

"Bani!" His name rang out imperiously.

He sought the speaker from his saddle.

A gnarled old soldier, his skin as weathered as the hide of an elephant, was examining him.

"I am Bani of the house of Hacaliah," he said haughtily.

"Address me as 'Sir!' and dismount. Immediately!"

The boy stared. The man wasn't even an officer.

Bani sat up straighter. "Take me to your Commander, my lord Oebazus," he snapped.

The next instant he was sprawling in the dust.

"On your feet," a leather sandal prodded him, "and follow me."

His knees and elbows ached. But he got up. The old soldier didn't bother to watch him. Instead he marched toward one of the low buildings. There was nothing he could do but obey. Until, he vowed, until he saw Oebazus.

Across the hot grounds he was led into a long narrow barrack.

"That's your bed," the soldier pointed to a cot with a straw pallet, "and there," he hauled a box full of garments from under the cot, "are your clothes." An unbleached smock and turban were tossed at him.

"Into it!"

He undid his crimson girdle, and removed his linen tunic. The smock and turban were coarse upon his flesh.

"Come with me!"

Again he had to follow. But at least he would have a sword in hand. Which one of these divisions was his? Cavalry he hoped. And where could Oebazus be. Had he not expected him?

"In here."

Bani found himself in a sort of shed. A familiar odor greeted him. Leather, metal, oil, rags. . . . He might have been back in his uncle's stables. Only no Chobi awaited him.

Instead four men, no, boys, stood stiffly at attention. Each held a lance in one hand, and a rag in the other. Bani gasped. They had been polishing the lances. No better than servants.

The old soldier ignored the boys. He took a lance from a rack on the wall. "This is yours," he handed it to Bani. "See that it shines." He pushed the dismayed boy down upon a bench. "Get to it!" And to the others, he barked, "Back to work!"

Instantly the four were at their benches, rubbing vigorously.

Bani gawked at the soldier's back retreating from the shed. He sought the four boys, but they took no notice of him. He started for the door.

"I wouldn't if I were you." Without raising his head, one of the boys hissed, "Old Crocodile might be just outside."

As Bani hesitated, one of the other boys whispered, "Let him alone Arioch. Let him learn the hard way."

But Arioch persisted. "Sit down," he urged, "he'll be back when you least expect him. And you'd better have the lance shining."

"I'm no servant!" Bani's eyes reddened.

"Oh ho," a third boy looked up. He was a Susian. His dark skin glistened with sweat. "Your Excellency. Pardon us."

"Summon my lord Oebazus," the fourth boy joined in. "None but the Arga-Pat himself may talk to his Lordship."

"Oebazus is my friend," Bani glared. "Wait, I'll show you."

"Don't be a fool," Arioch said. "The Arga-Pat doesn't even know we're here."

"I tell you," Bani began. . . .

"All right, then you know him," Arioch agreed. "We all know him. But it doesn't count for anything here. You're in the army."

"You mean you know Oebazus, too?" Bani was shocked.

"Our fathers do. We are to be Guardsmen, like you," Arioch said.

"Like this?" Bani pointed at the rag.

"It's part of it. Now hurry, before Crocodile comes back."

"Crocodile?"

"He fought in Egypt. Besides, they say he looks like one." Arioch grinned.

"Crocodile," Bani muttered, and the name made him

feel better. He found his bench and rag. Slowly he began to polish. But the lance refused to shine. He rubbed harder. Still the metal lacked luster.

"Try this," Arioch shoved a container at him. "Dip your rag in it." Bani obeyed. "Now polish. Now with the dry rag."

The first rag turned black. But under the dry cloth, the weapon began to glow. Bani rubbed harder. Soon the long brass pole sparkled all over. Now he started on the golden pomegranate upon its top.

At least he was to be of the first battalion of the Immortals. He stole a glance at the others. Arioch's lance also had a pomegranate. He was glad it was Arioch.

Suddenly "Crocodile" was back. Bani stood with the others, although reluctantly. The old soldier filed past each boy, examining his work. He took the lance from Bani's hand, inspected it, and threw it to the floor.

"I said polish, not wipe."

"I did."

Once again he was on the ground. His head rang from the blow.

"Speak when you're bid." The soldier growled over him. "Up now, and back to work. One more word of insubordination from you, and you'll be flogged. The four of you," he barked at the others, "to your divisions."

Left alone, Bani's eyes filled with tears, but he would not let them fall. Outside, trumpets blared, voices shouted drill commands, weapons clashed. What would his uncle have said of his treatment? And why hadn't Oebazus welcomed him? Nehemiah had made arrangements with the Arga-Pat. Was this really the way it was in the army?

He remembered Jadon, and the cool dim room, pricked with shafts of light. After all, it had not been so unpleasant at school.

His arms ached with rubbing, and his head with that blow. How long he worked he could not tell, but suddenly Crocodile was back. And with Oebazus!

Bani stood happily and saluted. Now, now Crocodile would get it.

But Oebazus ignored him. "Is this the disobedient soldier?" he asked.

"Yes Sir," Crocodile said.

"The charges!"

"Refusal to dismount when ordered. Spoke without leave. Refused to address me as 'Sir.'"

"A bad soldier." For the first time Oebazus confronted Bani. "Assign him to kitchen duties after hours."

"Yes Sir." Crocodile saluted.

Oebazus returned the salute, wheeled, and left.

Bani watched with horror as Oebazus disappeared. Was this his friend, Oebazus? This stranger who had stared at him as though he were a heap of dirt? His head swam with disbelief. But Crocodile gave him no time to reflect.

"After me!" he commanded.

Numbed, Bani followed. The sun, high in the heavens, glared angrily at him. The men at drill did not so much as throw him a glance.

Beside a squad using wooden shields and pikes, Crocodile halted. Immediately the Sergeant in charge cried, "Hold!" The squad stood at attention. The Sergeant saluted.

"A new one," Crocodile said.

"Yes Sir!" The Sergeant saluted. Crocodile returned the salute, and left.

"Take a shield and pike, and fall in!" The Sergeant pointed to a wagon nearby.

Bani stood at the end of the line. Now he would see action.

"To the left, march!" The line swung leftwards and forward. But Bani's feet had not heard. He was facing left, to be sure, but four paces behind the others.

"To the right, march!"

He ran to catch up, stumbled over his pike, fell. The ground shuddered about him. No one, not even the Sergeant, said a word. But Bani knew each man was aware of him. Humiliated, he got up, joined his line in time to about face.

For the next half hour, the boy twisted and turned; wheeling left, right, backwards, and forwards. His head and limbs creaked and groaned. Sweat poured down his back and from under his armpits. But he gritted his teeth. Never again would he disgrace himself before these men. Gradually, his body, tired as it was, began to obey orders more easily. He moved with his squad, doggedly, but correctly.

At last he was marched back to his barrack. He sank on his bed, wondering as he did how the others managed to sit upright. Too tired to look, he did not see them tying on leg armor.

Someone shook him. He opened his eyes. Arioch arched over him. "Put these on," he had his armor from his box beneath his bed. "And hurry."

In a daze he obeyed.

Just in time.

A trumpet blew. He was outdoors again, marching in formation to another part of the Citadel.

At home he would be drinking a glass of cool fruit juice. Acratheus would be waiting outside. At worst, there would be a few lines to learn. What would the assignment be today? Another prophet? Somehow, in retrospect, homework no longer seemed irksome.

"Halt!" Automatically his feet came together.

"In battle lines, fall in!"

He was facing another squad. Each pike pointed forward. Each shield covered the whole of each man's chest. All knees were protected.

Now, Bani realized dully, he was indeed to see real action. And he was so terribly tired.

Again a trumpet sounded. The lines moved forward: the pikes threatening, the shields raised to just below the eyes.

"Charge!"

He tried to surge forward with the others, but his feet were like lead. Suddenly the skies tore apart. The sun blazed. A loud yet distant clap of thunder exploded in his ears. Then with a shudder, light and noise vanished.

Bani was stretched out on the ground for the fourth time that day.

So began one of the most gruelling weeks of the boy's life. Instead of songs and good fellowship around the campfires, Bani did scullion's work around the kitchen fires. Between drill and battle maneuvers, he polished and polished. So exhausted was he each night that his straw pallet might have been the softest of cushions.

Shabbat embraced Bani that week as sweetly, he thought, as his Mother might.

He had always had some affection for this holy seventh day, mainly because he could be with Nehemiah. There were the prayers, the walk to Jadon's in the afternoon, the discussions. But more often than not he had fretted, longing to go fishing in the Ulai or gallop across the surrounding plains, had longed to be like Persian boys, unrestricted, free. . . . But not this Shabbat, which was like refuge found again, a kind of sanctuary where no one could reach him. He revelled in the fragrant cleanliness of his bed, his clothes, his food. And the violent pace of life in the Citadel was broken. No one could order him, neither Oebazus nor Crocodile; no one could keep him from thinking. For days, he realized, he had not been able to think: this, above all, had shocked Bani. For days he had not been Bani but instead a mechanical thing, who did what he had to do. He couldn't, come to think of it, remember enjoying the air, or sun, or stars during the six days at the Citadel.

At Jadon's he now listened with keener ears, saw with clearer eyes. Amos, of whom Jadon was speaking, seemed almost to stand before him, gaunt, burning with God's fire, demanding absolute justice, as pure and irresistible as a well-spring. Why had Jadon's words not meant so much before? After all, he had memorized these words. For the first time he realized his lessons were also the lessons for older men too. Thoughtfully he repeated the command of the Prophet to himself:

"But let justice well up as waters
And righteousness as a mighty stream."

What would the Crocodile have made of such an order?

Sundown came too quickly. An hour after Shabbat, Bani was back at the Citadel. Would he survive another week?

To his surprise, it was not so hard. He had learned to obey immediately and to say 'Sir.' Lances, pikes, shields, swords, were more manageable. And his body didn't get in his way anymore.

By the end of the month of Teveth he was mounted. At home in the saddle, he was as soldierly as the older men. By Shevat, he had knocked down an 'enemy.'

In Adar, he practised shooting backwards from the saddle. First with bow and arrows, then with a sling. By the beginning of Nisan, he was allowed to carry his own lance.

He and Arioch marched side by side, their long gleaming weapons with their golden pomegranates marking them as first battalion men.

How proud he was! He could almost forget those drills beneath the sun. But not the humiliations. These would burn forever.

Thursday evening, the last evening he was to sleep at the Citadel, he lined up for inspection. He had no idea who would be the guest of honor.

The trumpet sounded the royal salute. Artaxerxes himself moved down the ranks. Bani dared not twitch a muscle.

"At ease!"

He brought his lance down smartly. His eyes sought the King. Artaxerxes was mounting the platform of the fire-altar. As the King held a torch on high, he bowed his head in prayer. All except Bani leaned their brows against their lances.

"May Ormazd and the deities who guard my house bring help to me," Artaxerxes cried, "and may Ormazd protect this province from slavery, from decline, from lying: let not war, nor slavery, nor decline, nor lies, obtain power over this province. That I hereby commit to Ormazd with the deities who guard my house."

He lit the pyre upon the altar, remained with bowed head, then stepped down the stone steps. With Oebazus behind him, he moved out of sight.

The next day, Bani was called to the castle of the Citadel. Oebazus awaited him. He stood rigidly at attention before the Arga-Pat.

"At ease!"

Bani could barely relax.

"You may sit, Bani." Oebazus pointed to a bench.

Only then did he look at Oebazus.

"Do you still want to be a soldier?"

The boy flushed. He hadn't expected the question. "I, I'm not sure Sir."

"You were a little while ago." Oebazus waited. "You could be a good soldier."

"I?" He had been called a 'bad soldier.' And by Oebazus himself.

"Needed a little help at first," Oebazus said grimly. "But you learned fast. Remember Bani, when you return to Susa, your lance is waiting. There will always be a place in the Immortals for you." Oebazus stood.

"Thank you Sir," Bani was on his feet.

The Arga-Pat grasped the boy's shoulders. "Farewell, Bani, and take good care of your uncle. Bring him back to Susa." He paused. "Bring him back to me, Bani. He is my dearest friend."

The boy nodded, bowed, and left. But, he decided, adults were the strangest creatures. First, Jadon. Now, Oebazus. That these men should think he could influence Nehemiah in any way, either to go or to return. . . . As for taking care of him, that was the most ridiculous notion of all.

The First of Iyar, before the sun was up, Bani was mounted on his mare, beyond the Ulai, with around him the carts, horses, and men of the expedition to Jerusalem, drawn up in marching order. The escort was not so small after all, since it comprised two whole cavalry divisions. The white metal shields of the soldiers glinted faintly in the dawn which cast a ghostly aura over the men. In the rear, wagons bulged with provisions. Ten of them bore the royal seal, gifts from Artaxerxes himself. Everything seemed ready. Yet the trumpet gave no signal.

"Bani!"

The boy wheeled his mare in the direction of the voice. It was his uncle.

"Ride back across the Ulai. See what is keeping Master Jadon!"

"Very good."

He picked his way carefully through this other part of Susa. Its warehouses and granaries and markets were already astir. On the Royal side, however, his mare's hooves were overly loud in the stillness. As he was about to turn towards Jadon's, he reined in his horse. A pounding of hooves startled him. Around the corner one-humped camels swung directly at him. He remained rooted to his spot in the middle of the road.

They might have been soldiers. Some carried lances, others swords. Dark capes billowed out behind them. Expert riders, each man seemed tied to his camel. But who were they? Before he could move, they were passing him, their dromedaries swerving away from him with ease. It was difficult to see them, for their capes covered almost half their faces. Besides they rode so furiously.

The last of them was in front of him. He, too, swerved, but as he did the boy stared into two cold blue eyes. It was a fleeting sight. He might have been mistaken, except that a red jewel burned above them, a third, and in some mysterious way, an evil eye.

Icy fingers pressed down upon Bani's spine. Who was this man? Why had he sought an audience with the King. And why on this of all mornings was he rushing out of Susa? What terrible danger had to be averted?

The sun chose this minute to stream across the sky: golden-edged shears cutting the grey cloth of dawn. Bani shook himself. He was silly. What possible connection could there be between the stranger and Nehemiah?

He urged his horse forward. But he had no need to go further. A wagon, heavily-laden, and tightly-covered, was rounding the corner. Seated on it was Jadon.

Jadon, he thought, must be carting his whole house to Jerusalem. Strange. He had not expected the teacher to care about things. Certainly not about household furnishings.

5

Once the expedition got under way, the stranger of the red jewel faded from Bani's thoughts. There was too much that was new: fording the Tigris, crossing the marsh-lands of Sumer, and finally the arrival in fabulous Babylon.

Bani rode wherever he pleased. To his surprise and delight he found himself jogging alongside Jadon's wagon. Delight, because the teacher made so much come alive. When, for instance, they had crossed the Tigris, he had pointed southwest. "Ur is down there, Bani," he said. "Ur, where our Father Abraham was born."

Bani was interested. "Was Ur as beautiful a city as Susa?"

"More so. Wealthier, too. The most civilized spot in the world." Jadon paused. "And now," he added, "Ur is a shadow."

Three days after fording the Tigris, they came to Babylon on the Euphrates. For Bani who had believed Susa the center of all splendor, Babylon was a revelation. Her might had been broken, she was only a satrapy of Persia today, but much of her glory remained. Her mighty walls, though broken by Darius, still filled the onlooker with awe.

As for the Sacred Area, Bani could hardly believe his eyes. Temples to so many gods! But most of all the Temple Mount! Huge stone steps mounted one upon the other, with a stairway winding around the outside to the very top! Though they showed the scars inflicted by Xerxes, it was more magnificent than anything in Susa. A tower of Babel, Jadon had murmured.

The day after they arrived, Nehemiah took Bani to the court of the Satrap, the governor of the province. To get to it, they rode through evenly-laid out streets, into the Temple area, and through the Ishtar Gates.

A long festival avenue led them to the Palace. Bani rubbed his eyes. Were those gardens about the palace hanging in air? No, as they approached, he saw square terraces, one upon the other, rich with tropical shrubs and plants. The roof of the palace was also covered with lush vegetation.

On a throne of gold the Satrap awaited them. Before him were heaped sacks, flasks, casks of palm wood, and jugs. On a scale, stewards weighed silver and gold.

The Satrap descended the steps of his throne and greeted the Cupbearer of Artaxerxes. "Welcome, my lord, welcome."

Nehemiah bowed courteously. "Many thanks, my lord. I bring you greetings from the Great King." He handed him a rolled up parchment.

The Satrap kissed the scroll. "This way, my lords," he escorted them up the steps.

Bani stood at Nehemiah's side. Though the two of them were in court dress, they were drab compared to the governor of Babylonia. His turban was edged with gold and jewels. His hair, long and flowing, was heavily anointed. And his long linen tunic dazzled with precious jewels. According to the law of Persia Satraps retained half of the tribute they collected: both for their own maintenance, and the expenses of state.

"Taxes, my lord," the Satrap waved to the victuals and coins. "Our great King, you know, is supplied with one third of all his food needs, from Babylon alone. We must not let one crumb or drop fail his treasury."

Nehemiah nodded, his face grave. Bani's mouth puckered. This man, Jadon had told him, owned eight hundred stallion, sixteen thousand mares, thousands of Indian hounds, and a fortune in precious metals.

"The merchant Tabalis," a steward announced.

Tabalis was short and bald with a round paunch. Like all Babylonians his linen tunic reached to his feet, his wool, over it, came to his knees, and on top of this a short white cloak covered his shoulders and chest. The end of his walking stick was carved in form of a rose. Behind him slaves bore flasks, casks, and a small wooden chest.

Tabalis bowed before the throne.

"Read!" The Satrap commanded a scribe.

"Two casks of honey," the Scribe began.

One of the slaves set down two casks.

"One of wine."

Another slave deposited a cask.

"Two flasks of oil of sesame."

These two were presented.

"One hundred darics of silver."

The chest now joined casks and flasks.

"Inspect them!" The Satrap commanded.

Immediately two stewards bent over the produce. A third opened the chest, and expertly counted each coin.

"Well." The Satrap tapped his foot imperiously.

"All there my lord." The third steward announced.

Tabalis wiped his brow. The slaves grinned.

"You may go," the Satrap waved the merchant away. Tabalis bowed, and with his slaves, backed out of the hall.

As the offerings poured in, the morning passed. Different names, different men, but the main tax was grain and silver. After hours of this, Bani could barely make out sound or figure.

"The farmer Mazares!" Vaguely he heard the name.

Bani focussed hard on the newcomer. Ah, here was something odd. No slaves followed. No produce or chest were evident. The farmer himself walked poorly, as one who had not recovered his balance.

"Read," commanded the Satrap.

"Barley, two sacks," a scribe began. "Wheat one sack, two silver darics."

Mazares remained standing, silent, as though deaf.

The seconds ticked away ominously. Suddenly Bani realized he was watching a new scene.

"Well!" The Satrap glared.

Still Mazares was silent.

"I see no wheat. I see no barley . . . and no silver." Bani shivered at that last.

"Your Excellency," Mazares tried to speak. He spread his hands helplessly. "I am a sick man."

"We are not interested in the state of your health."

"If you will give me time, Your Excellency . . . ?"

"Your taxes are due, today."

"I have no coins or produce, Your Excellency. I have been bedridden, unable to work."

"How many sons have you?"

"No!" The man cried. "Please, my lord, I shall pay it all, and more. . . ."

A whip cracked. A red streak appeared on Mazares' face.

"Answer our question!"

"Three." The man wept.

"You shall deliver up two of them. If they do not bring enough on the slave market, we shall take the third."

They led the man away, still weeping. Bani's stomach heaved, as it had before the bleeding Makrian. He dug his fingers into the flesh of his thigh. Suddenly a strong hard hand gripped them. Nehemiah, seated, was steadying him.

After a sumptuous, and, for Bani, an unending feast, he and Nehemiah, left the Palace.

"My lord," Bani began eagerly as soon as they were outdoors, "how shall we find the farmer Mazares?"

Nehemiah studied his nephew. His eyes clouded. "We cannot find him, Bani."

"Not find him?" What then did the pressure of his uncle's hand mean? Had that not been a promise to help?

"I can't ask in there." Nehemiah nodded to the Palace. His lips twitched. "They would not understand."

"Let them think what they will." Bani dared to raise his voice.

"I am Artaxerxes' Cupbearer."

"You said we are Jews, my lord."

Nehemiah paled. "So we are, Bani."

"Then let justice well up as waters and righteousness as a mighty stream."

"Bani," Nehemiah spoke harshly. "We are in Babylon."

"Does justice change in Babylon?"

"Justice does not; but language does. Bani, you can challenge me without fear of punishment, because we are both Jews, and you speak what I cannot deny; the word of God. As the prophet Nathan did before David, or Elijah before King Ahab. But neither you nor I can speak this way to the Satrap."

"Why not?"

"Because he would not understand." And as the boy drew back Nehemiah leaned towards him from his saddle.

"Listen, Bani," he said, "what we have seen is evil. If it happened in Jerusalem, I would spare no one to uproot it, for Zion must be redeemed with justice, if she is to be redeemed at all . . . But here, though I should trumpet it to the heavens, no one would listen. . . ."

"We heard, my lord," Bani whispered.

"We! We are as much slaves outside of Israel, as Mazares," Nehemiah said sadly. "Come, Bani, we must go back."

They rode at a trot down the wide Avenue of Festivals and through the Sacred Area of Babylon. Among the many temples, the Mount spiralled upwards insolently. But Bani could not see beauty anywhere, now. Ah, then Nehemiah was not as powerful as he had thought! Nor was the God of Israel what Israel believed—all-powerful. Evil filled His world, and He did nothing. Why then did Amos speak in His Name?

"Bani, look!" Nehemiah pointed to the Temple Mount.

Upon the stone steps, the farmer, Mazares lay. A woman, squatting at his side, tugged at him.

Bani slid from his saddle. "Mazares," he called, rushing to his side.

"You know my husband, my lord?" The woman raised a tear-stained face.

"No, I mean, yes." Bani could have wept for joy. "I saw him in. . . ."

"Bani!" Nehemiah interrupted. "Silence."

A ray of hope that had lightened her eyes faded. Her

head drooped. Again she tugged. "Mazares, come, my husband, we must go up."

"Where must you go, woman?" Nehemiah asked.

"To pray, my lord. To beg for mercy."

"Of a stone idol?"

"Of Bel-Marduk, the great god of this Temple," the woman replied, outraged.

"Save your breath, woman." Nehemiah bent to hand her a purse. "Here, take this and redeem your sons."

Her hand trembled. The purse fell at her feet. "Who are you?" she whispered. "A spirit . . . ?"

"I am His servant." Nehemiah raised his head, and his face was radiant. "The servant of God."

"What is your God's name, my lord?"

"The God of all heaven and earth." He paused. "We call Him Adonai."

"I have never heard of Him," she said, puzzled.

"No," Bani laughed. "Of course you haven't. No one in Babylon has." He leaped into his saddle. "Come, my uncle. Let us hurry. We must get out of here. We must leave Babylon behind us."

6

■ ■ ■
■　　■

From Babylon they continued their way between the Tigris and the Euphrates into the Desert of Mesopotamia. Charchemish would be their next important stop.

Jadon, as usual, was full of stories. To the right, on the Tigris, he said, was the city of Asshur, while to the north was Nineveh. These had been the two main cities of the Empire of Asshur. From them Asshur had ruled many lands, had exiled the people of Israel, and with the insolence of power, had plucked up whole populations and resettled them in Samaria. Their kings had challenged God Himself. And now that empire, like Ur of Chaldea, or Babylonia, had vanished. Asshur was less than these poor villages where the natives quarried grindstone. Nineveh's chief claim to fame today was the King's Road that crossed her land.

And what of Israel, Bani asked? What of her glory?

Israel was eternal, Jadon said emphatically. Were they not returning to rebuild? Who would revive the dust of Asshur?

Bani did not argue. But he was not convinced. Artaxerxes, with a twitch of his eyebrow, could undo anything they might build.

Some afternoons, when their meat supply was low, Bani would join in a hunt. There was but one restriction for such outings. He must never go off by himself. He wanted to protest. Had he not trained at the Citadel? Was he not as good a soldier as the others? But one look at Nehemiah cut short his speech.

On one of these afternoons Bani rode off with a group. Hardly any animals were about, the hours flew by without a catch. They were ready to return to camp, when they spied a herd of wild asses. With a whoop, they made after them.

The soldiers herded the wild beasts by riding round and round them, groups of riders relaying each other so that the operation could be continuous. Bani watched. He didn't enjoy this hunt, and he was thirsty, too. He tilted his water skin, without result, for it was empty. He searched the plains. Not too far off, it seemed, were some bushes. That meant, perhaps, water nearby.

No one noticed his departure, and he did not bother to call out to them. He was sure to be back before being missed—or so he thought.

It was, however, much farther than he had imagined. By the time he arrived at the clump of bushes he was hotter and thirstier than he had been, and was exhausted. Fortunately there was water, and both he and his mare were able to drink their full.

Tempted by the coolness in the shade of the bushes, he decided to stretch out and rest there for a minute or two. He hobbled his mare, lay down, and fell asleep.

When he woke it was dusk, and very quiet. He searched the horizon. In the distance he thought he saw

points of light. He would have sworn they were in the opposite direction from camp, but since they were the only
lights, he mounted and cantered off towards them.

There were indeed two centers of light. That meant
two fires—not the dozen or more of his own camp. Some
sixth sense warned him. He dismounted, and leading his
mare, he advanced cautiously.

At the edge of a group of bushes, he hobbled his horse
again. Then he crawled forward on all fours.

The wind blew directly into his face, and the stench of
camels, struck him full-force. As he rounded a shrub, the
camp came into view. On a spit over one fire, meat was
broiling. A man watched it broodingly. Around the other
fire some sort of meeting was in session.

At least two dozen men, their backs to him, made a
semi-circle around the fire. One, obviously their leader,
was addressing them. The backs of the others concealed
him.

"As soon as we cross the river, Balikh," he was saying,
"we shall do it. This is our last chance before Charchemish."

"But how, my lord?" someone asked.

"An ambush?" a third voice suggested.

"In these flat lands?" another spoke up.

"Besides they outnumber us," a fifth reminded them.
"And they are trained men."

"You don't understand," their leader said. Bani
searched his memory. Somewhere, he had heard that
voice before. He would have liked to stand, to peer over
their backs, but he dared not move. "We are only interested in him," the familiar voice went on. "Without him
they can do nothing."

The camels stirred. The fat sputtered into the fire.
Somewhere an owl hooted.

Bani trembled. Whom did they mean?

"What does my lord suggest?" Again the question was asked.

"We must consider the man," the leader said thoughtfully. "He is arrogant." He paused, reflectively. "He is used to special attention, and he is fearless."

The heads of the semi-circle bobbed in agreement. "We shall use his weaknesses and strengths for his destruction."

"Do you think we are still unseen?"

"Yes. We have kept our distance of four miles from them constantly. And we do not travel by day. There is not even the dust of our dromedaries to reveal our presence."

"The meat is done, my lords," called the cook, who had been turning the meat.

With one accord the semi-circle of men stood up. Covered from head to feet in dark robes, they looked like so many evil spirits in the light of the campfire. But their faces were exposed. Bani could see their black pointed beards. They were swarthy men, although not as dark as Susians.

Now they gathered round the roasting flesh, accepting chunks of meat upon their short daggers. But their leader remained by the other campfire, his head bent in thought.

Bani watched him, his heart pounding, his suspicions aroused. Yes, it had to be that one. Suddenly the man raised his head.

Across the black-tipped tongues of fire, two ice-blue eyes stared at him. Above them a red jewel blazed, as though kindled by the leaping flames . . . Of course. Bani had known all along. It was he, the stranger.

The boy's mouth was as dry as the desert's sands. He was sure the man saw him. But as the eyes remained fixed, he realized they saw nothing, for the man was lost in thought, absorbed in his plans.

Carefully, slowly, Bani inched backwards. One knee after another, back, back, to his horse. He sensed before he saw his mare. In spite of his terror, he had wits enough to lead her gently away into the desert's blackness.

It was only when he was sure he was at a safe distance that he mounted. The two lights of the camp still pricked the night. Four miles, that one had said. Three and a half, anyhow, from where he was, and directly opposite. All he had to do was to take his bearings from the two fires.

After a few minutes, even that was unnecessary. Not too far from him were dozens of lights. He could barely believe his eyes. For these lights were moving, and in all directions.

He rode quickly towards the nearest light. It was Hanani and a soldier; Hanani with a torch, the soldier, with a trumpet. As soon as he came into view, the trumpet rang out. The torches, for that is what the moving lights were, turned back, converging upon the camp.

Hanani led him directly to Nehemiah. Jadon was at his side.

Not even the torches could tint the pale brow of his uncle. Nehemiah's hands clenched and unclenched. Then they covered his eyes for a heartbeat.

"My lord," Bani began timidly . . .

Nehemiah was in control of himself now. "You disobeyed orders Bani," he said sternly.

"I, I fell asleep."

"You went off by yourself."

"Yes, my lord. But I didn't intend to stay more than a minute. Besides, I must tell you. . . . I discovered another camp. . . .

"Go into my tent." Nehemiah interrupted.

"But listen . . . you must . . . please . . ."

"Immediately!"

Bani obeyed. As he bent beneath the tent's flap, he heard Jadon plead, "Softly, Nehemiah. You are too distraught. Wait till morning."

There was no answer, except for his uncle's footsteps. Bani tried again. "Let me tell you," he began, "what I saw and heard. . . ."

"Silence!" Nehemiah seized him in a grip of iron. "You have broken the rules of this camp. You have disrupted every man and beast. And you have . . ." he stopped, "No never mind! Only this you will never do again." He seized a leather thong, raised it, and brought it down on the boy's back. Bani was flogged as he had never been flogged before.

Bani uttered no sound, but his hatred grew with each whiplash. Then, when it was all over he crawled out to sleep beneath the sky.

What a fool he had been! He could have stayed in Susa. Well, he would get back the first chance he could, even if it meant returning to old Crocodile.

Next day Jadon asked Bani to drive his wagon. Wanting to refuse, Bani accepted. After all, the seat of the wagon was cushioned and, aching as he was, his saddle was torture.

As he climbed into place, it occurred to him that the wagon was as tightly covered—really sealed—as when it had left Susa. How careful the teacher was with his possessions! One might think he had a treasure concealed beneath the wraps.

Jadon said nothing that morning. Quietly the boy and man jogged along. When they stopped for food, the two ate together. Hanani invited Bani to ride with him. Bani refused, and curtly. He could almost not bear to look at Hanani, or at the others. Everyone in camp must know he had been whipped. He would never forgive Nehemiah.

By mid-afternoon they reached the river Balikh, its waters flowing south into the Euphrates. The river was high. Bani had to give all his attention to the bullocks hauling the wagon. The water, however, did not reach the load. He heard Jadon's sigh as the animals strained up the banks of the other side. As he took his eyes off the bullocks, he found himself looking straight at Nehemiah. His uncle was watching him intently. And anxiously?

He felt the blood drain from his face. Cracking the reins smartly, he fixed his eyes upon the bullocks. When he raised his head a few moments later, Nehemiah was gone.

At dusk they camped in a grove of date palm trees. After his evening meal with the teacher, Bani decided to sleep with him as well.

As he lay beside Jadon, he asked how much of the journey had been accomplished, and how much remained.

"One third of the way still to go, Bani," Jadon replied, "and the most exciting part."

That came to over five hundred and thirty-five miles. Two months of travelling. How would he ever get back to Susa now?

"In another few weeks we come to the Great Sea," Jadon added, "and to her cities, Ugarit, Bybols, Sidon, the Satrap's seat. And then, then," the teacher's voice dropped, "then, Jerusalem."

There was one city missing. An important city. He rolled over on his belly. He must remember.

"What is it, Bani," Jadon asked. "What bothers you?"

The other camp. He had forgotten it in his pain and shame. Should he tell Jadon? Nehemiah? No, never his uncle. . . . Besides what could he say? He had heard men plotting. No name had been mentioned. And supposing it were Nehemiah? Did he really care?

How could Nehemiah have flogged him? How could he?

"Bani," Jadon whispered, "say the Shema. Then try to sleep."

He pretended he was already asleep. As for the Shema, he would leave that to Nehemiah. That and his precious Jerusalem.

A clatter of hooves woke him. Slipping quietly into his tunic, he went out of the tent into the misty dawn. A stranger upon a dromedary was addressing Hanani.

"Your message!" Hanani demanded.

"It is for my lord Nehemiah."

"I shall deliver it."

"What is it, Hanani?" Out of the veils of fog, Nehemiah himself appeared.

"A messenger from the Satrap Adeus, Nehemiah."

"From Sidon?"

"No, my lord," the messenger volunteered. "He is, was, at Charchemish."

Bani started. Of course, that was the city he could not recall. But now he understood. Jadon had not omitted it. Charchemish was on the Euphrates, not on the Great Sea.

"And what does Adeus desire?" Nehemiah asked.

"To meet you," the rider bowed from his camel. "He has been informed of your arrival, and for your great honor and his, would escort you himself unto Charchemish."

Nehemiah examined the man carefully. "Tell Adeus for me," he finally said, "we shall be close to Charchemish in about five days."

"But he has already left Charchemish two days ago. He planned to hunt on the way. He bade me ask you to take just a few fast riders for your escort. The rest of the expedition can catch up to you later, in Charchemish."

"Hmm," Nehemiah frowned. "We shall see. In the meantime," he addressed his cousin, "see to the man's needs, Hanani."

As the messenger was led away, no one but Bani and the sentry remained. The footsteps of the pike-armed guard as they raced to and fro were slow accents of doom in the boy's ear.

There was no doubt in his mind now. He had been right. Nehemiah was their victim. And this was an ambush. The blue-eyed plotter was clever. He had described Nehemiah exactly. "Arrogant, used to special attentions, fearless." There would be nothing unusual for the Satrap of Arabaya, a province which included Phoenicia, Israel, and Cyprus, to advance and escort the favorite of Artaxerxes. At least not in Nehemiah's sight. And surely he who had dared to ask the Great King himself for leave to go to Jerusalem, would not hesitate now. Certainly not with an escort of his own soldiers.

Nehemiah would be surrounded, killed.

Bani could see it all; those thundering hooves; the encirclement; his uncle's dead body.

He must warn Nehemiah. But how? How could he swallow his pride? How could he go to Nehemiah? He would be no better than a cringing puppy, come back to lick his Master after punishment.

He stumbled back to Jadon. The teacher was dressed, and just finishing his prayers.

"You were up early, Bani."

"A rider woke me."

"A rider?" Jadon's eyebrows raised. "From where?"

"From Charchemish. From the Satrap. So he says."

"You doubt it?" Jadon teased.

"I don't have to doubt."

Jadon's brows wrinkled. "What then, Bani? Speak plainly."

"I know. The man is lying."

"You are so positive," Jadon smiled. "How could you know?"

"I tell you I know." Bani burst forth. "That night," he felt his cheeks redden, but made himself go on, "that night I came back so late, I had discovered another camp, by accident, and there I heard the plot."

"Plot! What plot?" Jadon stiffened.

"To kill my, my . . . to kill Nehemiah."

"Bani!" Jadon dug sharp fingers into his shoulders, "this is no stupid trick. You aren't making this up?"

"Why should I make this up?" Bani wrenched himself free of Jadon's grip.

"Because of your anger." Bani opened his mouth. . . . "No, I know how hurt you were, my son." His lips twitched. "You are your uncle's nephew. The same anger, the same pride . . ."

"I am not like him," Bani cried, "and I am not making this up. I heard it. From the mouth of the same man I had seen in Susa."

"Describe him!"

"Black beard, blue eyes, a red jewel hanging from his brow, almost between his eyes."

For an old man Jadon moved swiftly. "Fetch Hanani," Bani heard him command someone outside his tent.

As the teacher reentered his tent, he threw a sharp glance at the boy. "You knew this all day yesterday," he said.

"I suspected it. I heard no name, not even the details

of the plot. Except it had to be before we reached Char-chemish."

The tent flap lifted. "Hanani," a soldier's head appeared, "is with my lord Nehemiah. He will be with you within the hour." The head disappeared.

"Come with me, Bani!" Jadon commanded.

"Where to?" He asked, knowing too well.

"To your uncle, of course." And without waiting for a reply, Jadon led the way.

The teacher pushed the Cupbearer's curtain aside unceremoniously. Nehemiah and Hanani, deep in conversation, did not hear them until Jadon spoke.

"My lords," Jadon bowed, "forgive us, but Bani has something to say."

All eyes focussed upon the boy. His tongue was as stiff as bark, and as dry. He kept his eyes on his sandals. At first his voice cracked, then gradually the words came more easily as he described his experience.

There was a pause when he finished. Then Hanani commanded as had Jadon, "Describe their leader!"

"Black beard," Bani said again, "blue eyes, a red jewel . . ."

"Geshem! Geshem the Arabian!"

"And this messenger?" Jadon asked.

"An Arab too. There is no mistaking them. You see," he turned and addressed Nehemiah, "I was right."

Bani's head jerked upward. So Hanani had not been fooled. Then there had been no need for him to seek out Nehemiah.

"Why didn't you tell me sooner, Bani?" Nehemiah asked evenly.

"You gave me no chance." Again his cheeks burned, remembering. Tears of shame pricked his eyeballs. He pivoted swiftly, and left the tent.

Later that day he was summoned to Nehemiah's tent again. To his amazement he found the three Captains, Hanani, and Jadon. This was obviously a council of war. Surely this was no place for him. He started to leave.

"Stay, Bani!" Nehemiah said.

"But you are busy."

"You are part of the Council today. Sit."

"I?"

"You have earned your place," Nehemiah said briefly, but his eyes held the boy's as firmly as a handclasp. "And now," Nehemiah addressed the others, "shall we fall in with their plans?"

"You know how many they have?" Narseh, one of the Captains asked.

"Bani?" Nehemiah waited.

"About two dozen."

"We can handle them easily," the second Captain said.

"Then I shall send their messenger back immediately." The others nodded assent. "And I and half a dozen men shall leave tomorrow." Again they nodded. "Narseh, you will be ready with your division."

"Yes, my lord. And all picked men."

"No," Hanani said to his cousin, "you must not go."

"Why not?"

"Something might happen."

"We shall be there first," Narseh assured Hanani.

"Still, there could be a mishap. And without you, Nehemiah," Hanani said sternly, "we are helpless."

"What do you suggest?" Nehemiah asked.

"Dress a soldier in your robes, have his head covered by a hood. They will not know the difference."

"And if he is killed?"

"You will be safe."

Nehemiah's lips had whitened. "And I shall have shed innocent blood, Hanani."

"Israel must be saved."

"Not through murder."

"There is no murder in war," Hanani said stubbornly.

"Is that why we are commanded to give a ransom for our souls before battle?" Nehemiah asked. "Tell him, Master Jadon."

The three Persian Captains leaned forward. Narseh's lips had parted.

"Killing is killing, whether in war or peace," Jadon said quietly, "but Hanani does not deny this. He is thinking of Jerusalem, not of Nehemiah."

"I too am thinking of Jerusalem, my Master, Jerusalem shall be redeemed in justice, or,"—his voice shook—"not at all. I shall not send another where I dare not go. Our God, and not Geshem the Arabian, decides my life or death."

Jadon bowed silently. The Captain sat back thoughtfully. Hanani reddened.

But Bani glowed. It was good to be born of the House of Hacaliah. It was good to be a nephew of this man. Yes, in spite of all that had happened, it was good. . . .
The messenger left that afternoon. At midnight armed soldiers rode out of camp. Under the cover of darkness, no one noticed an extra rider.

Exhilarated by the cold air, and the prospect of action, Narseh and his men galloped across the plains. As the morning star began to fade, they came upon a double grove of trees.

"This is it," said Narseh and raised his hand. "We wait behind both groves. The horses in the middle. No fires. No movement. Whispering, yes, but nothing else."

"Fifteen here," Narseh checked off the soldiers, "to the right. And the other fifteen, over there, to the left."

"We are sixteen, Captain," a Sergeant observed.

"Impossible. I called for thirty." He stiffened. "Identify yourselves!"

A mare with its rider stepped forward. "No need, Captain," a youthful voice announced, "I am the sixteenth."

"Bani," someone whispered.

"Bani! No!"

"It is I, Captain. Bani of Hacaliah."

"By whose permission?"

"No one's, my lord."

"How dared you?" Narseh was furious.

"It is my uncle's life that is in danger." Bani said simply. "It is my duty."

"It is your duty to behave like a soldier. What will your uncle say?"

The conversation of the council rang in his ears. "He will say . . . but no . . ." Bani hesitated, "I do not know what he will say."

"You know, boy. At least you know what he will do. He will thrash you as he did the other night. And I shall approve."

Bani's hand whitened upon the reins. Was that a snicker behind him? Well let them. He didn't care. He had done what he had to. As Nehemiah had in the face of Hanani and Jadon.

"Join them!" Narseh commanded. "Now that you are here you must. But you have no part in the attack. Stay behind those trees at all times."

He trotted with the fifteen other men to the grove on the left. He would do exactly as he intended. Let Narseh rave. Let Nehemiah punish him. Let these men think what they would. . . .

But the soldiers about him accepted him as one of them. They shared not only their bread and cheese with him, but their water, too.

Lazily the sun struggled out of her night's shift. First her ribbons and streamers trailed across the sky, then she appeared in all her golden cloth. Fortunately it was cool among the foliage.

"Nehemiah will be over there by now," the Sergeant pointed southward, from where they had come, "waiting for the signal."

"Signal?" Bani was aghast. "But they will hear it, the Arabs."

"Hardly." The Sergeant grinned. "Look up." Bani obeyed. Only then did he notice a soldier in the tree top.

"He'll see the Arabs before we hear them. That's when he'll flash his shield."

"But they might see it too."

"Why should they? They'll not be looking for it. And should anyone notice a sudden brightness, it will be just the play of the sun. But Nehemiah will not advance until they come into view. The plan is for them to meet between us."

"And when do we attack?"

"Not until they begin."

"But they . . . they might kill my uncle before we can do anything. . . ."

"He should have sent a decoy then." The soldier shrugged his shoulders. "Hanani was right."

How quickly the camp learned what went on within the tents. And how little they understood Nehemiah. No one understood him, neither kin nor friend. Neither Oebazus nor Hanani nor himself perhaps?

A horse neighed. Instantly a soldier was at its side, soothing it. How much longer could they wait before all the animals would get restless and betray their presence?

Suddenly the tree above them rustled. The soldier on its topmost branches faced north. For a heartbeat, he appeared to be straining to see something in the distance, then, quickly, he swung about, secured his footing, and raised his metal shield above his head.

The Sergeant signalled. The men mounted their horses, reining them in tightly. Over each of their shoulders hung quivers of arrows, and across every man's knees lay a huge bow. They were ready.

Bani knew better than to move. But he lovingly fingered his bow.

They heard the dromedaries before they saw them, and as the thunder of their approach became louder and louder, the hoof-beats of the horses from the south became audible.

The men bent over their mounts. The moment was almost upon them.

Louder, louder.

Now! Between the branches Bani saw the camels, the horses, and there, Nehemiah tall in his saddle, a perfect target.

"My lord Adeus!" Nehemiah called out.

"My lord Nehemiah!" How well Bani knew that voice. "Greetings!" The hood fell back, but only partly; yet enough to reveal the red jewel. Even in the shade of the grove, it glowed. "A special greeting."

To Bani's horror a lance hurtled through the air.

But Nehemiah was ready. He swerved. The lance thudded into the earth. The Arabs behind screamed a deadly scream. With curving swords, they swooped down upon the six Persians surrounding Nehemiah.

With this, the groves split apart. Arrows arched through the silvery air. Camels heaved, their heads flung back, then with another cry, this time of dismay and terror, camels and riders tried to escape.

These fleet ships of the desert cleaved the sands. But the arrows flew faster. Mounds of black stuff streaked with red dotted the plain.

Some Arabs, however, were untouched. Weaving from side to side, they eluded the arrows. One in particular, escaped, Bani saw him—indeed, he had eyes for no other.

Out of the grove, at an angle calculated to cut him off, dashed Bani. He neither saw nor heard the Arab behind him.

"Geshem," Bani shouted, "Geshem, I am coming for you. I, Bani of the House of Hacaliah!" His reins hung on his mare's neck. He snatched an arrow from his quiver behind him, set it in his bow, and drew back, taking aim.

"TNNNNG!" The arrow found its mark in Geshem's right shoulder, but as it did, a sword arched downward, and Bani's bow was slashed in two. He heard the whir of air as the same sword swished upward again.

This then was his last moment. "Shema," he began instinctively . . . and closed his eyes against the downward curve of iron . . .

But instead there was a thud. He opened his eyes. A camel, riderless, was pulling away.

"Bani!" The reins of his horse were caught. A powerful arm encircled his shoulders as both his mare and the stallion next to him drew up.

In the distance, Geshem, the arrow still embedded in his shoulder, fled, a lone rider. Bani leaned against Nehemiah, suddenly weary.

Narseh galloped up. In the heat of the battle, he spoke bluntly. "Nehemiah," he called out, "the boy came on his own. Let no one but the boy be blamed!"

"Bani!" Nehemiah exclaimed, holding him close. Bani

could feel the tremor that shook his uncle's whole body, and was resigned to take his due. Nehemiah never accepted explanations. He would certainly accept none now. But to Bani's amazement, he heard his uncle ask, "Why, Bani? Why?"

"It was my duty," he said.

Nehemiah released him. "How so, Bani?" He asked quietly.

"I am a son of Hacaliah." The boy's hands clenched at his side. "He," Bani nodded towards the tiny figure receding into the horizon, "he threatened me when he threatened," he paused, "when he threatened you. Still," he added firmly, "the Captain is right. I was not ordered here."

Nehemiah did not stir. For some heartbeats he was lost in his own thoughts. His stallion snorted. "Yet," the sound seemed to awaken him, "according to Narseh, you have been a bad soldier. Let him decide your punishment."

The Captain started. His glance swept from Nehemiah to Bani and back to Nehemiah. "Not I, my lord," he refused. "He is your nephew!"

"No," Nehemiah said, "I could never punish the son of Hacaliah for remembering he is Hacaliah's son. But," he added grimly, "my nephew knew the consequences of his deed. Let him accept them." He paused. "That too is the code of Hacaliah."

As they rode back to rejoin their camp, Bani might have been content. Except that Geshem had escaped. And he would have to help the cook until Charchemish.

That, after all, was a servant's chore.

7

At Charchemish the expedition rested. There was much to see: the citadels with towers and battlements, the stone beasts, two-headed, with wings and paws deeply carved, the Hittite weather god with his peaked cap. And Jadon talked about Ur of Chaldea, Asshur, Babylonia, then Hitti—all mighty empires once. As mighty as Persia now was. Bani listened and learned.

From Charchemish they went south, across the Orontes River, to the first city on the coast, Ugarit.

Bani was overwhelmed by the brilliance of Ugarit, and even more by the Great Sea itself. How blue it was, how vast! Jadon assured him there were other coastlines beyond his vision, and many islands among the sparkling waters. But Bani found it all hard to believe.

"Yet these are the least of God's wonders," Jadon said.

"What could equal this?" Bani demanded.

"Love. The love that sent you to your uncle's defense."

"Duty!" Bani snapped.

Jadon smiled. "We make up all sort of words for it, Bani. Duty, honor, pride. . . ."

From Ugarit they travelled to Byblos, the city famous for its manufacture of parchment. From Byblos it was not far to Sidon. This seaport had both a winter and summer harbor.

The Satrap, Adeus, entertained Nehemiah and Bani with a hunt in the Paradise. As they rested in the luxurious pavilion, Bani recognized the figures of carved bulls kneeling back to back. These same carvings rested on top of the columns of the Apadana at Susa.

How alike all these cities were. Jerusalem was probably no different from Susa, after all.

From Sidon to Tyre was but a few days travel. But they did not linger here. Nehemiah ordered them on with just an afternoon's rest.

They turned inland from Tyre. After a while, something happened. Bani could not describe it. Except that Jadon, Nehemiah, and Hanani were different. They even rode differently: spines stiffer, heads thrown back, eyes clouded.

Behind them huge cedars rose upon distant mountains. In the foreground one mountain, snow-crowned, towered above their heads.

"Hermon," Jadon said, "our northern border."

Then Bani understood.

He was in the land of Israel.

From here on his own history surrounded him. Mountains, rivers, cities, footprints, spoke to him out of his past. But they barely stopped. It was as though they had no time for any place but one. And the nearer they approached that one, the more rapt they became. About a mile from their destination, Nehemiah commanded the Captains to encamp until he should send for them.

Only Jadon, Hanani, Nehemiah and Bani proceeded. At night, as Nehemiah had planned, they arrived.

Jerusalem, starlit, rose before them.

At the foot of the holy Mountain the three men knelt and kissed its soil. On foot, Jadon leading his bullocks, they ascended.

The stars hung low above Bani's head. He could touch them, he thought, if he but stretched out his hand. Never had he seen such a sky.

What a pity Nehemiah had insisted on entering Jerusalem in the dark. Surely this city must be glorious to match such a heaven.

To be sure, he saw the broken walls Hanani had described. But Babylon's walls had also been smashed, without destroying her magnificence.

On the very top of the Mountain, before other walls, they paused. From between two bronze gates, about a dozen men emerged. With one accord they bowed.

"Welcome to the House of the Lord." A man in white stepped forward.

Nehemiah bowed. When his head lifted, Bani saw the tears. His uncle wept openly, without shame or embarrassment. So too did Jadon, and Hanani. The group parted, and the man in white escorted them inside the gates.

They were in the Temple.

This was obviously the Outer Court. At its end they mounted fifteen steps, passed through another set of enormous gates, and into an Inner Court.

All sorts of shapes bulked in the starlight. On one a fire glowed. Above them aloof and silvery, a building seemed suspended.

A tremor rippled down Bani's spine. First Nehemiah's tears. Now this. The Sanctuary, mysterious, sacred . . .

Nehemiah held a roll of parchment above his head. In the starlight, Bani saw Artaxerxes' seal. In a firm voice, Nehemiah said, "You know, my brothers, that God has kept our Fathers, Abraham, Isaac, and Jacob, in mind continually. For the sake of their righteousness, He has not left off the care of you. Indeed he has assisted me in gaining the authority of the King to raise up our walls and finish what is wanting in this, our Temple.

"I desire you, therefore, leaders and elders of our people, that you will in the first place put your trust in God, and in the second that you will be determined to build up our holy city, nor to interrupt our work, neither night nor day, but to use all diligence now we have this special opportunity for it.

"And do you, Eliashib, High Priest of our people, lay this letter from the King Artaxerxes before God."

Breathlessly, Bani watched the white-robed one accept the parchment. With no hesitation he strode into the farther part of this Inner Court, and up twelve steps into that silvery building. Where would Eliashib lay the letter? On the golden altar inside, or before the Holy of Holies?

When Eliashib emerged, he returned the letter to Nehemiah. "I have fulfilled the command of Nehemiah," he bowed.

"Thank you, Eliashib," Nehemiah said. "Now I can send this to Adeus in Sidon. If our enemies complain, the truth shall bear witness for us." He paused. "And, now," he added, "I am ready to be presented to Ezra, our Master."

Did Eliashib frown? Bani couldn't be sure. "As my lord commands," Eliashib said. No, he must be mistaken.

They trooped across the marble pavement towards one of many chambers beneath a colonnade. Eliashib turned the knob. The room, it seemed, contained nothing but chairs. These were ranged in semi-circles, opposite each other. Between the halves these semi-circles formed was one chair and a table. An old man sat there.

A very old man. All in white! Hair, beard that reached his chest, robe that covered him down to his ankles. A wide flat nose spread across his cheeks. But no one lingered over that feature. For above them two piercing black eyes scrutinized each man.

Nehemiah advanced towards him.

A yard before the table he bowed. The two, Nehemiah and Ezra, were face to face.

The old man stood up, slowly. He leaned on the table to do so, but once erect, he was steady. With measured steps, he came from behind the table.

"My lord Nehemiah," he said, but so low, Bani could barely hear him. "Is it truly you?"

Nehemiah's lips trembled. "Bless me, my father," he said, "for these my eyes, which have looked upon God's House now behold the face of His messenger."

"Then the Lord bless you, indeed, my son," and Ezra's voice was stronger, "may He strengthen your hands to purify our city and His people."

Did the men about him stir, Bani wondered? But he had no time to consider it. Jadon now stood before Ezra. "My master and my teacher," Jadon said, "bless your servant, Jadon, too."

Delight illuminated the old Scribe's face. "Jadon," he cried, "that I have lived to see you, my son." But even as he spoke, the light faded, and a stern tongue continued. "Has the shepherd left his flock? Are God's people to live without Torah?"

"As my master commanded me," Jadon said, standing erect, "so have I commanded my students. The flocks in the fields of Susa are not untended."

"Then blessed be your coming, Jadon," and Ezra opened his arms and embraced him. "We can use you in the pastures of Jerusalem."

"We bring good sustenance," Jadon said. "If you are not too weary, I would show you." And as he spoke, he invited the others outdoors.

With Ezra between Nehemiah and Jadon, they left the Temple proper. Before the walls, on the Temple grounds, Bani saw Jadon's wagon, still tightly sealed.

What would Ezra want with furniture? Bani wondered. What nonsense to offer such a man rugs, or vases, or, and he smiled to himself, more chairs! Bani was embarrassed for Jadon as he uncovered the wagon. But when the heavy cloths were removed, he gasped.

Visible to all in the starlight were scrolls and tablets. In a flash Bani remembered, and remembering, understood. The shelves of Nehemiah's library . . . emptied of so many of their treasures.

He blushed, ashamed of having wrongly judged his master.

Ezra approached the wagon. His fine old hand trembled as it lifted parchments and tablets.

"For the Temple?"

"For Israel," Nehemiah replied. "For all who hunger."

"Nehemiah," Ezra cried, "God has indeed sent you. Only he who first mends the mind can mend the body." And he filled his arms with parchments, pressing them lovingly to his breast, as a mother does her child.

"No, Ezra," Nehemiah replied, "we must do it together. Mind and body." Then he turned to the others. "There is much to be done, and time is short. If we take council here we can make our plans before our enemies have a chance to muster their forces." His hands dropped sharply at his side, "My lords," he continued, "I will speak to each of you."

"We are yours to command, Nehemiah," Eliashib said, "we shall meet with you tomorrow."

"Tonight!"

"Tonight?" They were all astounded. "But surely it can wait for the dawn . . . besides, you must be weary."

"Tonight!" Nehemiah repeated. "And furthermore, no one but you must know of my arrival. I command you to keep secret my presence in Jerusalem."

"But why, Nehemiah?" Eliashib asked.

"So as not to alert our enemies."

Bani saw Eliashib and another exchange glances. An unspoken message passed between them.

"Nehemiah . . ." Eliashib began . . .

"It is my command," Nehemiah said curtly. "No one but you are to know."

Bani could not help smiling to himself. This was something new for these Jerusalemites! These men would have to get used to Nehemiah and his driving energy.

As though his uncle had heard his thoughts, he turned upon him. "Bani!"

"Yes?"

"You are to retire!"

"May I not be of assistance?"

"In time." Nehemiah said grimly. "But now, to bed. Hanani, if you please, show him the way."

"As you say." Hanani bowed. "Come with me, Bani."

Bani followed angrily. He was tired, yes, it was true. But that was still no reason for being treated as a child. Had he not proved himself against Geshem?

When would Nehemiah realize that his nephew had grown up?

8

The Governor of Judah's mansion was next to the Gate of
Ephraim, that was all the boy knew when he fell asleep.
When he awoke, it was to a large and airy room.

Nehemiah stood before him.

"My lord," he sprang up.

"It is early, Bani. I am just coming from Ezra's chamber. I shall sleep for a few hours, and resume my meet-
ings. You will join me then. Until I give you permission,
you are not to leave this house."

"I must remain indoors!"

"For as long as is necessary. You would be marked as
a stranger. It might point to our presence. If any of the
elders arrive while I am asleep, you shall greet them in
my stead."

"Very good." He threw off his cover.

"And Bani . . ." Nehemiah paused at the door.

"Yes?"

"No Persian garments; just that tunic, girdle, and sandals. They are laid out for you. We are in Jerusalem now."

He dressed quickly. He would be his uncle's representative; a sort of Vice-Governor. A glow of pride and satisfaction warmed him. Yet last night, he had been sent to bed like a baby. Would he ever understand Nehemiah?

A servant waited for him outside his door. "This way, my lord," he bowed, and led him to a magnificent dining room. Ebony chairs, carved and mounted with ivory, were set around an enormous table. In a corner a bronze statuette, with long thin lips and bulging eyes, gawked at him. Bowls of deep reds and blues held anemones.

Clearly the former Governor of Judah had wanted for nothing. It was exactly as it had been in those other cities he had visited. He should have been relieved. But somehow, he was disappointed.

He might never have left Susa. True, in the Temple last night, he had been moved. He had almost forgotten who he was, except that he was a Jew. Perhaps it had been the stars, the silvery Sanctuary, or the altar, always burning in God's honor. But this morning he was again Bani of Hacaliah. He was singular, as he had been back in Susa. Nehemiah's nephew, his deputy.

How he wished the servant would announce someone.

But the morning sped by without a visitor. Nor, for the hour after Nehemiah arose, did anyone arrive.

"Shallum ben Hallohesh!" At last a Jerusalemite had come.

Nehemiah received him in his Room of Audience, on a carved throne. Bani stood at his side.

"Your excellency," Shallum bowed. He was tall, and wiry. All angles, with skin the color of parchment.

"It is late," Nehemiah said grimly.

"I am ruler of the Zion district of Jerusalem," Shallum reminded Nehemiah tersely. "I have my duties."

"So," Nehemiah studied the man. "And what of the others?"

Shallum shrugged his shoulders. "I suppose it does not suit them to be up all night."

"It is more than that." Nehemiah leaned forward. "Tell me, Shallum, why is there such disunity in Judah?"

"So you know that already."

"After last night, a blind man would. Ezra and Eliashib, is it not?"

"Eliashib is a fool!" Then noticing Bani, he gasped, "What is the boy doing here?"

But Nehemiah did not share his outrage. "He is my nephew. He must learn," he said curtly, closing the topic. "But about our High Priest, what does he want?"

"Peace."

"The desire of a wise man."

"At all costs?"

"What costs? Speak plainly, my lord."

"Idolatry for one!"

Nehemiah heaved out of his chair. Bani stared. "Shallum ben Hallohesh," Nehemiah said sternly, "do you know what you are saying?"

"Too well," Shallum said grimly. "Oh, Eliashib would not serve idols; but," he paused, "he would welcome those who did."

"Plainly, I command. These are serious accusations. Who are those he would welcome?"

"The Samaritans! Those pagans Sargon brought from Babylon after exiling our brothers." His contempt was icy. "These, their sons, have lived so long on land they never inherited, they think all goes with it, even our God. Side by side with their Marduk or Baal."

"Then where was Ezra?" Nehemiah frowned. "Why has he endured this?"

"Ezra did what he could. He rid Israel of these pagan wives and husbands once. But they have returned." He paused. "Ezra is, after all, an old man; and no ruler. He is a teacher, an interpreter of Torah. These men are shrewd, and too strong for him. It is time you came, My lord."

"Yet Ezra made no mention of this last night."

"With Eliashib there? Meshullam, their friends . . . ?"

"Then I must speak to him alone."

"Yes, you must. Ezra is waiting for you," Shallum said.

"Who told you that?" Nehemiah asked sharply.

"All who love Israel, have been waiting for you, Nehemiah, or for someone like you."

"Eliashib ben Joiakim!"

With the announcement of the High Priest, Shallum's face sharpened; like a hawk's Bani decided.

The High Priest entered the Room of Audience, every inch of him an aristocrat. His collar and turban were edged in gold. Perceiving Shallum, he stopped abruptly.

Shallum bowed to Nehemiah. "It is time I went, my lord Governor."

Eliashib drew back as Shallum departed.

"I see that the High Priest of Israel disapproves of the ruler of the Zion district of Jerusalem," said Nehemiah.

"He is a bigot!" Eliashib snapped.

"How so, Eliashib?"

"Only Israel is pure, according to men such as Shallum," Eliashib sneered. "His holiness Shallum can't even bring himself to talk with a non-Jew."

"Talk, my lord, or marry?"

Eliashib paled. "What has that man said of me?"

"Much, my lord, I shall not hide it," Nehemiah said evenly, "but not that the High Priest has married outside of Israel." Nehemiah stood. "Need I remind the High Priest of God's House that there is a bare remnant of us left, and only if we remain Jews, strong and dedicated sons of God, shall we save ourselves and our nation."

"Israel is eternal!" exclaimed the High Priest.

Bani started. Jadon had once said that, and just as emphatically.

"Israel, the people of the Covenant," Eliashib went on, "will never die."

"Your position, Eliashib, seals my lips," Nehemiah said grimly. "But let me remind you, a covenant is a two-way affair. We, and especially the elders who lead Israel, must fulfill our part."

"Exactly," the High Priest agreed, "and how can we, if we neglect God's House? The people do not pay the temple tax, neither the priest's due, nor the Levite's."

"I have come to establish His House, in all His ways."

The High Priest bowed. "Then may your hand be blessed in all its work. Shalom."

"Shalom," Nehemiah replied, escorting the High Priest to the door.

Bani's head swam. Geshems were threatening from without, and discord was within.

"Well Bani," Nehemiah asked, "what do we do now?"

"Me?" Bani could hardly believe his ears. "You are asking me?"

"You heard Shallum. You also heard the High Priest."

"But, I don't understand. Shallum must be wrong. Eliashib is a leader. He must love Israel."

"It does not always follow. There are disloyal men among all classes. There's Tobiah . . ." Nehemiah spat out the name like a curse.

"Who is Tobiah?"

"Governor of Ammon. Calls himself an Ammonite. Yet he was born a Jew."

"But Eliashib is High Priest." Bani persisted.

"Yet it is rumored his grandson, Manasseh, is to be married to the daughter of the Governor of Samaria." Nehemiah paced the room. "Pay attention, Bani. Keep your eyes and ears open. Especially these next few days. All this concerns you."

"I shall, I shall," he said eagerly.

"As it concerns all Israel," Nehemiah added.

"Oh." He was disappointed. He had hoped Nehemiah had singled him out.

During the next day the Elders came and went. Even Ezra with Jadon were among the visitors. In the presence of the Scribe, Bani observed, Nehemiah sat in a plain chair.

On the third day an unexpected visitor was announced: "Sanballat, Governor of Samaria."

Bani saw fury tighten Nehemiah's features. Who had dared to disobey him? But by the time Sanballat entered, the Governor of Judah had composed himself.

The Samaritan was the handsomest man Bani had ever seen: tall, with a broad white forehead and a high-beaked nose, he wore his beard in long parallel curls. He was splendidly dressed, wearing a purple cloak of finest Babylonian wool, and precious jewels flashed on his ears and fingers.

"Greetings, Sanballat," Nehemiah said.

"My brother, greetings!" Sanballat repeated, with a cordial smile. "I had hoped," he added, as he accepted a chair, "that I would be honored by a visit from you. I am not so far from Jerusalem, you know. But as the days passed fruitlessly, I decided to come to you."

"Duty before pleasure my lord Governor."

"Duty? Ah, yes, I have no doubt there is much to be done. I trust you will permit Samaria to assist Judah."

"Wherever possible."

"Good." Sanballat twisted a curl of his beard on a be-ringed finger. "I am happy to hear it. I feared, Nehemiah, that you might be one of those narrow provincials."

"Are you talking of my brothers of Judah?" Nehemiah asked coldly.

"Your brothers! But no! You who come from the most worldly court of the world, the court of the Great King himself, surely you could not regard these people here as brothers."

"I am brother to every son of the Covenant." Nehemiah stood, too impatient to remain seated.

"Your loyalty does you credit," said Sanballat, without moving. "Of course, in truth they are our brothers, these narrow men."

"How so, Sanballat?"

"How so? But, we of Samaria are also Israelites, Nehe-miah. Samaria is a part of the land of Israel."

"Indeed!" Nehemiah frowned. "And has Samaria ac-cepted the God of Israel?"

"We must accept Him; seeing He is the God of the land upon which we live. After all, it is His due."

Nehemiah shook his head sadly. "You do not know Him, how can you accept Him, the only God."

Sanballat smiled triumphantly. "There, you have said it. And if He is the only God, he is God of all men, and is therefore ours."

"All men may claim Him, yes; but only Israel is partner to the Covenant."

"The Covenant? What exactly does that mean?"

"The keeping of Shabbat; the protecting of the weak, the poor, the widow; the cancellation of debts."

"Then you will find no men that keep this Covenant.

They keep no Shabbat here in Jerusalem. As for protecting the weak," Sanballat smiled faintly. "Wait, and you will see."

Nehemiah paled. "Is it as bad as that?" he whispered.

"I don't know what you call good or bad, my lord Governor," Sanballat said, standing face to face with Nehemiah. "You speak of the weak, the poor, the widow. These may need protection in your sight. For practical men, they are the realities of life and as such are God's handiwork. To change what He has decreed surely constitutes disobedience to God." Sanballat smiled good-naturedly. "In any event, I have not come to discuss philosophy with you. I am here to extend the greetings of Samaria to you, and her offer to help repair the Temple. In return, we ask only to bring our sacrifices to God."

"And shall the bleating of calves of sacrifice drown out the cries of the weak? No, Sanballat, none can have a part in rebuilding the Temple, except the sons of the Covenant."

"Then what of the Nethinim who serves in the Temple? They are not Israelites. All know these are the sons of the Gibeonites."

"Who have accepted the Covenant."

"The Covenant!" There was no pretense of a smile now. "Why do you prate of covenants, when I tell you few, if any, know it? Why should the men of Israel who desecrate Shabbat be better in the eyes of God than Samarians who do not keep it?"

"Not better. I have not claimed we are better." Nehemiah spoke to himself. "Who knows whether we still deserve to be the chosen people? But thanks to the merit of our Fathers we have been chosen. And now we have a duty, a purpose."

"And that is?" Sanballat sneered.

"To fulfill His commandments. Or, if you prefer, to be His witnesses upon earth," Nehemiah said. "Nor do we have a choice in this, unless . . ."

"Unless . . . ?"

"Unless we are ready to die."

"That is a possibility," Sanballat said menacingly.

Nehemiah eyed the Samaritan. "You may think so; but we Jews do not. That is the difference between us. Israel shall never die. She has been punished, yes, that we know. You are the living example of the punishment."

Sanballat was not put out. "Nehemiah," he said, "I had hoped you would not force me to these words; but you have given me no choice. I asked you for a part in the rebuilding of the Temple." He paused. "Now, I demand it."

Nehemiah's hand grasped his sword. His face was white as death.

"Be calm, Nehemiah." Sanballat's eyes were slits. "I would not do anything so foolish, if I were you."

"You had better leave."

"I go. But not until I finish what I have to say. We are both governors. My voice carries as much weight in Susa as Nehemiah's. More in Sidon, with Adeus. Ammon is also my brother."

"And Arabia," Nehemiah said icily. "Especially Geshem, the murderer."

For the moment Sanballat lost his control. He flushed, then said aloud, too loud, "I know nothing of Geshem."

"I will not argue the point," said Nehemiah with a contemptuous laugh. "But now that you have given me this warning, listen carefully, Sanballat. You shall not enter Israel. Neither you nor any man who rejects the law of Israel. As for the disobedient sons of the Covenant, if I do nothing else, I shall purge them of their evil ways.

You say they desecrate the Shabbat, oppress their brothers . . ." Nehemiah did not take his eyes from Sanballat. "I promise you, not a spade shall be turned on Shabbat in Judah, nor one victim's cry arise to the God of Justice. Not while I am the Governor of Judah." He paused. "Can you assure me of the same for Samaria?"

"I assure you of only one thing, Nehemiah ben Hacaliah," Sanballat said composedly. "Either you admit Samaria into the House of your God, or there shall be no House to Him. Good day to you." He turned to leave.

"His House shall stand, Sanballat," Nehemiah called after him, "in spite of Samaria, or Ammon, or Arabia."

Sanballat paused, and in that pause, Nehemiah added, "Tell your allies, yes, even the men of Judah who traffic with you, that I, Nehemiah, shall establish it, even if I must do it alone."

Sanballat left the room. Nehemiah, standing there, looked as immovable as a statue.

Bani's heart thudded in his chest. How fearless Nehemiah was! How majestic!

Hanani entered. "Was that Sanballat, Nehemiah?" His forehead wrinkled with disbelief as he put the question.

"No other!"

"But how? Who told him you had arrived?"

"The troops, perhaps. Camped out there, they might have been discovered."

"Or Eliashib?" Hanani said slowly.

"Or Eliashib." Nehemiah repeated. Then slamming one fist into his open palm, he added, "Tonight, Hanani. We move tonight."

"What are your plans?"

"We must strengthen Judah. First her walls. Then her people."

"But Sanballat? Tobiah? They will make mischief."

"Of course; but what can they do if we are strong and united? Tonight, Hanani, we shall inspect the walls. Just you and I. . . ."

"The Elders . . . ?"

"No one, except perhaps Shallum."

"And I," Bani said. "May I not go?"

Nehemiah hesitated, then said, "Perhaps, yes, Bani, why not? Yes, Bani you should go with us. You are growing up."

Bani controlled his face. He must not show his emotion. He was a man. Nehemiah, himself, practically admitted it. But if he could, he would have flung his arms about his uncle. Never, never since he could remember had he been so pleased.

That night, they inspected the walls of Jerusalem. Nehemiah rode upon a mule. He, Hanani, and Shallum walked. They went out by what Hanani called the Valley Gate, southward to a very large pool, the Dragon's Well, then to the east towards the Dung Gate. Here they halted.

The moon was out; the stars in full attendance. The broken walls cast fearful shadows, and where the Gates had stood, rubble bulked.

No one said a word, but led by Nehemiah they continued southeast to the Fountain Gate and northward to what was left of the King's Garden. Here heaps of stone and rubble were so high, the mule could not proceed.

Nehemiah dismounted, and the four of them squeezed through into the grounds where once King David and his attendants must have sought the shade and fragrance of green trees.

In the garden there was both a small pool, and on the

northwest side, a spring, the Spring of Siloam. In the center, an enormous stone staircase led up, to the House of the Warriors of the King.

Bani could picture David and his mighty men among these trees. Joab, Abishai, Ira, and the wild and reckless sons of the King; Ammon, Adonijah, Absalom. . . .

Yet it was in ruins. And from what he had seen through the windows of the Governor's House, Jerusalem was hardly a Carchemish or Sidon; certainly not a Babylon.

He should have been shocked, he supposed. But he wasn't. Here, he felt, was the true Jerusalem; here in this abandoned garden of King David. Here it was, as though he felt the footsteps of history marching in his veins.

And in a way he could not understand, Jerusalem, no, the whole land of Israel, became more precious to him because of these ruins. These tangled branches and weeds clutched at him, binding him to them, to his past, and to himself. More closely than the Temple's stone, this garden's foliage stirred him. He lifted his head to the night wind. He would breathe in every drop of this antique air.

He had no time to linger, as he desired. Already they were headed back to the Valley Gate. Outside its rubble, they remained in the valley for at least an hour. Nehemiah viewed the city, over and over again. Then silently, at his signal, they reentered Jerusalem, and returned to their homes.

On his couch Bani tried to recall the fleeting minutes of the garden, but could not. Sadness, an aching sadness, so deep it crowded out all other feeling, filled his being.

Early next morning messages went out from the Governor's House to the whole district of Judah. All were to assemble in the Broad Place that was before the Water Gate of the Temple; the area between the east wall and the southeast part of the Temple.

With Nehemiah, Bani toured Jerusalem by day. What the boy had realized in the King's garden by night, was borne out by the light of the sun. Jerusalem was a shambles.

There were not many homes, and these, for the most part, needed repair. So too the Temple. Her chambers, her walls, her columns, were cracked and peeling. The garments of her priests threadbare, patched.

For all one could tell, it might have been only yesterday Nebuchadnezzar had destroyed the city. Gashes in the road, uprooted pavements, debris, told the story of that attack and defeat; and now one hundred and forty-two years later, of despair.

"Hanani did not exaggerate," Nehemiah commented, "did he Bani?"

"It is not Susa, my lord."

"Nor is it the dust of Asshur," Nehemiah snapped, "nor the ruins of Nineveh." Then as Bani stiffened, Nehemiah pointed to the Eastern Gate of the Temple, "that is a reminder of Susa, and of the goodness of Cyrus who sent us back to our homeland."

"That gate!"

"Look closely, Bani. It is a copy of the Apadana."

So it was. The fluted columns, the bulls perched on them, back to back . . . for a heartbeat Susa beckoned to him. How would it be to be back; hunting with Acratheus; even the lessons in that dim room with Jadon. . . . But Jadon was here. He returned to the present with a start.

In two days people began streaming into Jerusalem. They came from all parts of Judah. From Jericho and Tekoa; from Meronoth and Gibeon; from Mizpah and Zanoah; from Beth-Cherem and Beth-Zur; from Keilah and from the plains of the Jordan River. They came on donkey and on foot, on wagons and, the wealthy few, in their fine chariots, or on prancing steeds. If there were un-invited, they were not noticed among such a multitude.

Together with Priests and Levites, the Judeans gathered in the Broad Place. In the forefront, before a platform, elders and rulers of the various districts stationed themselves.

The dais was empty. Behind it, on the Temple walls, guards marched.

All, even the nobles and rulers, chattered away. Why had the new Governor ordered this assembly? Not since Ezra's arrival thirteen years ago had they been summoned here. Then they had been called upon to repent. Many recalled that sense of purification, of rebirth. But this newcomer was probably no teacher, like Ezra.

All sorts of opinions were offered; gloomily, and with outright groans. For the most part, they agreed it meant either higher taxes, or a mustering of an army for a Persian campaign. One, or the other, or both, would be severe. Else why should the Governor have to announce it? Weren't the Rulers capable?

When the trumpet sounded all talking ceased. Heads craned, as from the Temple itself a group emerged. Nehemiah, flanked by Ezra and Eliashib appeared. Behind them walked Hanani, Jadon, and Bani.

For Ezra's sake, Nehemiah moved slowly as, together with the High Priest, he mounted the platform.

The three men surveyed the people.

No one stirred. Every eye was focussed on Nehemiah. What kind of man was he? What would he do? Their very lives might perhaps depend on his words and deeds.

"My brothers of Israel," Nehemiah began, "I am your new Governor, Nehemiah ben Hacaliah."

Nehemiah! Who had not heard of Nehemiah? That

man in distant Susa, more myth than man, who could reach the ear of Artaxerxes himself.

"Behold," Nehemiah exclaimed, "behold the evil case that we are in!" He waved to the Temple behind him, to the Temple Mount, and to the whole of Jerusalem. "Jerusalem lies waste, her gates are burned with fire."

As though by signal, the older women answered aloud. "Woe," they cried, and "Woe unto the city of God. We are a reproach unto the nations. We are a mockery unto our enemies. . . ."

But Nehemiah would not let them lament. "No," he cried vigorously, "no tears, no woes! We shall build up the walls of Jerusalem. We shall no more be a reproach, neither to God nor man."

"But my lord," a voice asked, "how could we build, since we are surrounded by enemies?"

"We are surrounded by God."

"What will the King say? He is surrounded by our enemies."

"For example, Geshem the Arabian," someone added.

"Or Tobiah the Ammonite!" To Bani's surprise it was Shallum who cried out, shaking his fist angrily. Those around him fixed scornful eyes upon Eliashib. But the High Priest remained aloof. Just a patch of red on his cheekbones, above his beard, proved that he had heard.

But Nehemiah had heard. "What, an Ammonite?" he laughed. "Do not call Tobiah an Ammonite. He is neither Ammonite nor Israelite. He has given up the ways of his people to ape what is not his. He is a slave; a slave to fear and ambition."

"A slave," Eliashib could no longer contain himself, "Tobiah is the Governor of Ammon, Nehemiah. Surely his rank deserves our respect."

"Pharaoh was a King, High Priest." Nehemiah faced Eliashib. "Haman was a Prime Minister. Would you respect them?" And as Eliashib was silent, Nehemiah turned back to the people. "He is a slave. Let him be called by his true name."

"Tobiah the Slave!" The people shouted as one, delighted. "Tobiah the Slave, the Slave. . . ."

A horn sounded. The crowd fell silent. At the farthest edge of the crowd, an Ammonite, horn in hand, had blown the blast. Now he shouted, defiantly, "Then beware of slaves! Especially this slave of Artaxerxes. Tobiah the Slave shall inform his Master."

"Of what?" Nehemiah demanded.

"That you are rebels. That you will build up what he has not commanded."

"Has he not?" Nehemiah challenged. "Or has your Master the Slave not heard?" And as the Ammonite remained speechless, Nehemiah addressed the Judeans. "My brothers, hear me, and take courage. Artaxerxes himself has commanded me to build up the walls of our holy city, to restore her beauty, and to bring peace to our city of peace. Do not fear these barking dogs, though they bear the name of Governors. Our God has softened the heart of Persia, first of Cyrus, then of Darius, and now of Artaxerxes. Our God has brought us back from exile. He sent you His Messengers. First Zerubbabel the son of David, and Joshua the Priest; then His Prophets, Haggai and Zechariah, and then Ezra our Teacher who stands before you."

"You listened to them," Nehemiah continued. "You rebuilt God's Temple. You raised families, planted, harvested. And then," he paused, "then you became frightened." He raised his hands upward. "God calls to you again. This time, we must complete the task. We must set

Jerusalem firmly upon her foundations. For Jerusalem is
the heart of Judah. And if the heart is whole, the body
shall be whole and produce a healthy seed."

"What does Ezra say?" someone demanded.

The old Scribe, Ezra, stared over the sea of heads into
the distance.

"My children," he began, "you know how God has
spoken to us—to Abraham, to Moses, and to all Israel
from Sinai. We are not only His people, but more, we are
His partners, we have signed a Covenant with Him. Therefore, we must live for that Covenant. We must declare the
oneness of God, His Fatherhood, and man's brotherhood."

The horn blared, shrill, angry. The crowd pivoted as
one man. Furious hands reached for the Ammonite.

"No!" Ezra cried, and each hand held. "No," he repeated, "turn to me, and let there be no violence."

"See the man of peace," the Ammonite cried, from the
rear of the crowd. "See the man of peace," he repeated
sneeringly. "Man's brotherhood, he says. Yet he, Ezra
himself, drove wives from their husbands because they
were not Israelites."

A lump formed in Bani's throat. How could one talk of
brotherhood, and drive one's brother or sister, away?

But Ezra remained serene. "Brotherhood of man de-
pends on God's Fatherhood. Shall we declare the oneness
of God," he asked, "while worshipping false gods? Shall
we pray to one Father in heaven, and bow our knees to
Chemosh, to Baal-Peor, to Baal-Zebub? Ask yourself, Ammonite, which of your gods would you abandon for the
sake of Adonai? Which god did those wives surrender?
And which did they teach their children to surrender?"
And as the Ammonite was silent, Ezra continued, "We do
not trick God. We do not bargain with His Godliness. He
is our only God or He is not our God. We are the sons of

His Covenant or we are the betrayers of His Covenant." He paused, breathing deeply. "We are men, mortal, sinful. There is no man who does not sin. But our Shema, our 'Hear O Israel the Lord our God the Lord is one,' is the beginning and the end of our Covenant. If you break other laws, you can make amends. But if you break either this beginning, or this end, you cease to be Israel."

"Israel! Such glory!" the Ammonite taunted. "Defeated, dragged into exile, her Temple in ashes; this," the Ammonite pointed above Ezra's head, "is not what your King Solomon built. His was a Temple. Yours is a shadow, like yourselves. Israel, ha! Who would want to be Israel now?"

Bani looked at Nehemiah. Would he permit this to go on? To his amazement, Nehemiah was not only smiling but Ezra and Eliashib were smiling as well. As though each guarded a secret that put him above such taunts.

But Bani could not smile. The Ammonite spoke no falsehood, that he knew. He had seen Susa, Babylon, Ugarit. He had seen the august power and wealth of Persia. Why should his Uncle and Ezra and Eliashib want to be Jews? What made the Covenant so special? It had not protected them against their enemies. If only they would answer this Ammonite! Not for the Ammonite's sake, but for his own.

The horn blared again.

Nehemiah raised his hand. Instantly a detail of soldiers closed in and dragged the Ammonite before the dais.

"Three times, Ammonite, you have disturbed the peace of the Temple Mount," Nehemiah said. "I sentence you to be flogged. Ten lashes."

The Ammonite paled. "You shall pay a hundred for each one, Nehemiah."

As though he had not heard, Nehemiah contined, "When you get back to Ammon tell Tobiah the Slave that neither he nor any pagan has a portion or right or memorial in Jerusalem."

As they led the Ammonite away, Nehemiah called to the Judeans, "Are you ready, O Israel, to build the walls of Jerusalem?"

"We shall build, Nehemiah!" the people shouted, and raised their hands as though taking an oath. "We shall build."

"Then our God shall prosper us. Let all who can, remain."

So it was that not only the citizens of Jerusalem joined together to raise up the ruins, but all those who had come from the farthest cities and districts of Judea.

Eliashib was the first to take up a shovel. Immediately around him other priests clustered. They began at the Sheep Gate, the northeastern gate near the Temple.

Nehemiah approved. More, he set them the task of building the portion that extended to the Towers of Hammeah and Hananel. To help them, he assigned the men of Jericho, and next to these, Zaccur, the son of Imri.

Around and around the city Nehemiah went, dividing the task. To Bani's horror, even the daughters of Shallum labored. In Susa, such girls were not even permitted outside their homes.

But Shallum seemed unconcerned. With his robe tucked up under his girdle, he went about his task near the Tower of the Furnace as vigorously as if he and he alone were charged to rebuild the whole wall.

Like Shallum, the shepherds of Tekoa toiled. The wall beneath their hands grew like Jonah's gourd. Their portion at the Northern Wall was completed first. Promptly then, they joined the Nethinim at the Water Gate.

Thus the task began splendidly. Because there had been a famine in Judah that year, Nehemiah took it upon himself to feed the workers, and for the first time in many months some tasted meat.

Nehemiah should have been pleased. But Bani knew he was worried. Many times during these days, Nehemiah would stare out towards the north expectantly.

At the beginning of the second week it came. A soldier in a leather tunic brought the news. "They are there," he reported, "four miles to the north."

"How many?"

"An army."

"Why are they waiting?"

"For reinforcements from Arabia and Ashdod."

"Ashdod too," he paused, "and what of Ammon?"

"Already there."

"Then it is to be a real attack."

"They are very angry. Especially Sanballat."

"How so?"

"He said so."

"His very words, man."

"What do these feeble Jews," he spoke before the army, "will they restore at will? Will they sacrifice, will they make an end this day, will they revive the stones out of the heap of rubbish seeing they are burned? Come, let us show them the will of Samaria."

"And his men," Nehemiah's voice was steady, "how did they answer?"

"Tobiah answered for them."

"Ah, yes, of course. I should have known."

"He was angrier than Sanballat. He has received your message."

Nehemiah's nostrils flared. "It was intended for his ears." And as the soldier was silent, he commanded, "How did this Slave whine?"

"Tobiah threatened. He said, 'Even that which they

■ 126 ■

build, if a fox go up, he shall break down their stone wall.' "

A group of Judeans had gathered by now. They were silent, watching Nehemiah, waiting.

For a while Nehemiah stared northward at that army he could not see. "A fox," he mused. "It is well put. Tobiah is a fox, sly, deceitful, like all traitors. . . ." Then as though noticing the knot of men about him, he asked, smiling, "Does the lion of Judah fear the nibbling fox, my brothers?"

"No, Nehemiah," they shouted joyfully.

"Then on with the work! If necessary we shall roar. Or rend."

With renewed energy they returned to the wall. But though Nehemiah mounted his stallion, he did not move. Instead he lifted his head heavenward as one who seeks an answer. For that heartbeat, the Governor of Judah was revealed. Weariness and anxiety grooved his face.

The boy at his side was both frightened and dismayed. How his uncle had thinned! Aged! As though Jerusalem were a sculptor who had fashioned a new body for him, or better still, had chipped away all marks of Susa.

Nehemiah lowered his head, bowing it over his mount. Then Bani heard him pray.

"Hear O our God, for we are held in contempt," Nehemiah said. "Turn back their reproach upon their own head, and give them up to contempt in a land of captivity. Cover not their iniquity, and let not their sin be blotted out from before You; for they had vexed You before the builders."

He lifted his head, breathed deeply. Suddenly he snapped his reins, and cantered around the wall. Bani kept pace with him.

It was an imposing sight. All Judeans united. Eliashib,

begirdled in gold, even as he sweated, laid stone upon stone. Goldsmiths, merchants, farmers, shepherds, rulers, nobles, elders, women, children. Many had taken up the refrain of the Levites. "Except the Lord build the House, they labor in vain who build it. . . ."

At the western wall Bani measured the height of the wall with his eyes.

"At least twenty-five feet, is it not, Bani?" Nehemiah said.

"At least."

"One quarter," Nehemiah smiled.

"We should be done, before they can stop us."

His uncle's smile faded. His lips pressed against each other. "They can never stop us, Bani. Don't you know that?"

"But still," he hesitated, "you are concerned."

"Concerned? No, Bani. Our God shall fight for us." He half-smiled now. "Who or what can prevail against Him? But that does not mean we must be idle." He paused. "We are men, Bani. His sons. We are expected to act like men; to plan like men."

"Then faith is not enough!" He blurted it out unthinkingly. After all, had he not heard Nehemiah's prayer?

"Without it we can achieve nothing. With it everything. But we must do, in order to achieve, that is the point." For a heartbeat the Cupbearer of Artaxerxes, arrogant and powerful, flashed before him. "Don't ever forget it, Bani. Let your deeds speak for you, and fear no man. . . ."

"And God? Shall we fear Him?"

"If you have cause," Nehemiah said grimly. "But," his grey eyes held the boy like a magnet, "if you do His commandments, why should you be afraid?"

9

■ ■ ■
■　　■

Sanballat and his allies attacked the next morning. It was
just a sortie; a warning to Nehemiah. Yet one of the sons
of Hasseneah was slain.

At the head of his troops, made up of young Persian
soldiers, Nehemiah drove them back, Bani at his side.
Once again Nehemiah had wanted to object. Once again
Bani could almost hear the command sending him back.
But the boy was no longer a petitioner. He had leaned
over his mare's neck; had almost dared Nehemiah to
speak. The Governor of Judah had paused; then as one
who must agree, had nodded.

Bani knew there would no longer be a question of his
position. With that nod, he had begun a new chapter of
his life.

They buried the son of Hasseneah that afternoon. Since
they could not lay him in his family's tomb, they put him
in earth on the mountain opposite Moriah. No one wept.
Neither Hasseneah nor his wife.

Briefly Nehemiah spoke. "Jerusalem, O Lord," he said,

"is Your altar; not only of the land of Israel, but of all the world. We, not lambs, are Your sacrifice, upon Your hearth." He picked up a clod of earth and poured it gently into the open grave. The clean scent of soil lingered in each nostril. "Jerusalem, your sons sanctify you with their blood." He raised his head to the blue sky. "Atone for us."

And as all the people cried, "Amen," Nehemiah declared, "Let us go up to our stations outside the walls. Your Captains are waiting to lead you. Only remember whom you defend: Jerusalem, your wives, your children, and," he paused, "the very future of Israel. Be strong and of good courage, and our God shall fight for us!"

They remained for a heartbeat with bowed heads. Then, with another 'Amen,' unspoken, but echoing within their hearts, they went, each man, outside the partially built walls of their holy city.

Evening came and passed. Night followed; for once a starless, moonless night. "No fires," Nehemiah commanded. "Let them have no guides for their arrows."

As all waited, encased in darkness, and their own thoughts, two men approached Nehemiah.

"Nehemiah . . . ?"

"Who goes?" Bani held his spear ready. Other spears made a half circle around Nehemiah.

"It is Eliashib and Meshullam."

"What do you wish?" Nehemiah asked sharply.

"A word." The figures of the High Priest and Meshullam the son of Berechiah were more clearly outlined now.

"At such a time!"

"Because of this time," Eliashib said.

A pause. "Very well then. What is so urgent?"

"Nehemiah, we desire to end this war."

"I, too, desire the end of it."

"Then give us leave to speak to them. They might listen to us."

"To the enemy?"

"If you call them that."

"They have slain your brother. What do you call them?"

"Nehemiah, hear us," Eliashib was pleading. "We are Jews like you. We love Judah, Israel, our Temple. Surely you do not think we would hurt Jerusalem?"

"Only the dregs of our people could do that."

"And I am the High Priest of our people," Eliashib said. "A son of Seraiah. Yes, of the very same family as Ezra. Yet I disagree with Ezra, and," he added after a pause, "with you. The Samaritans only wish a portion in our Temple."

"Pagans!"

"Who would come close to God."

"Who would profane His Name."

"But it would be a first step for them. Can you not see? If we allow them to be part of us, they will be drawn closer and closer to God. But if we reject them, they will never know God and will remain idolaters."

"Eliashib," Nehemiah replied, "I have heard you out, because I must believe you sincere. But ask yourself: Which of these Samaritans or Ammonites have given up their false gods?"

"It takes time, Nehemiah."

"We have no time. Can you not see? We are a small people, a remnant. Our strength is not in the sword. It never was. But it *is* here," Nehemiah touched his heart, "in the power of our faith, in the purity of our faith. If we allow idolaters in, they will adulterate our pure faith." Eliashib would have protested, but Nehemiah waved him aside. "No, it would be inevitable. People take from each other. We would copy them as we have, in the past. Have you forgotten Zimri, who worshipped Baal-Peor because of the Midianite women? Have you forgotten Solomon, who built high places for his foreign wives and their gods? Have you forgotten the women of Jeremiah's day who worshipped Neith? For Baal-Peor we were punished with plague; for Solomon's sins, Israel was split in two; for the idolatry of the women we went into exile. Are plague, disunity, and exile not enough? Or are your memories weak?"

"Nehemiah," Eliashib said, "I remember Ruth. Her blood flowed through David's veins."

"Then you must remember what she said. 'Your people shall be my people; your God my God. . . .' She came to Israel with all her heart and soul. Chemosh, her god, Moab, her land, the King of Moab, her father, all these she gave up completely. Have Sanballat or Tobiah or any of their people ever spoken thus?"

"Give them a chance," Meshullam pleaded. "Perhaps they would."

"I have met Sanballat." A pause. "Did not Eliashib know?"

"Yes," Eliashib said, "I sent him."

"Against my orders!"

"I would do it again, Nehemiah, for the sake of Israel."

"You take too much upon yourself, High Priest. I am the Governor. Remember that, in future. High Priest or not, I shall take measures."

When the High Priest spoke, his voice was so low Bani could barely hear his words: "You have the authority, Nehemiah, I shall not argue that. But you shall be judged, nevertheless."

"By whom?"

"By the future, Nehemiah."

"I prefer God, Eliashib. He searches the heart."

"The heart of man can err."

"What then should I use, Eliashib, seeing it is all I have."

"Then use it with humility, Nehemiah."

Yes, Bani thought, Eliashib had scored. Humility was not Nehemiah's strong point.

"Eliashib," Nehemiah said, "I pray I shall ever walk humbly . . . with God . . . and with His sons, but," and his words cut like steel, "I pray I shall never be humble before evil or treason. And now if you truly love Jerusalem, to your posts, my lords!"

With a stiff bow the two disappeared into the darkness.

Before dawn the combined armies of Samaria, Ammon, Ashdod, and Arabia attacked, their chiefs on horseback, in the vanguard of the foot soldiers. The battle lasted until noon.

Throughout the fighting Nehemiah could be seen on his mount, slashing, shouting, charging, rallying. It was almost impossible for Bani, and the rest of the young bodyguards to keep up with him. As the sun rose higher and higher in the heavens, the Judeans gathered new strength. Whether it was the memory of Hasseneah's son, or the example of their Governor, they pressed so hard, the enemy's ranks finally broke.

Nehemiah pursued them, determined to destroy all opposition forever. But as he ignored the foot soldiers he could have slain with one sweep of his sword, Bani realized he was pursuing one man only, was that man Sanballat? Or Geshem?

The fleeing horseman turned in his saddle. No, it was another—hard to discern, but unmistakable.

"Tobiah!" Bani shouted.

The horseman in fury bore down upon him. Yes, it was

the renegade Jew. Bani fixed his arrow, drew his bow, but as he was about to release it, another horseman swept down from another side. . . .

A red jewel flashed. A blazing knife seared the length of his arm. The air whirled with black arrows. He slid from his saddle. An abyss yawned to engulf him.

But before he disappeared into its depth, he heard his uncle's hoarse cry of despair: "Bani . . . Bani . . . answer me . . . answer me. . . ."

He woke in a darkened chamber. His right arm ached. His tongue was rough and thick.

"Bani." A cool hand touched his head.

"Water," he tried to say, but only a rasping sound came forth.

"Do not speak." Again the cool hand brushed him.

Afterwards, he had no idea how long afterwards, someone held a cup to his lips. He tried to drink, but half of the liquid spilled over his chin.

A strong yet gentle hand lifted him. The room whirled. Again he began to fall. But this time he was held tightly against a hard body. The smell of leather and sweat filled his nostrils. A beard pressed against him, and distinctly he felt a kiss on his forehead. "Bani, Bani," his name was spoken in a whisper, "Bani, get well, do not leave me, my child. Without you I am empty, Bani, empty . . ."

When he regained consciousness, Nehemiah was gone. A woman sat at his bedside. She attended deftly and silently. Jadon came to see him, and once Ezra visited him. But Nehemiah came not at all. Had that been a dream, that kiss, that anguish . . . ?

Once his strength began to return, he recovered rapidly. Then, one morning, he refused to stay in bed.

The woman left him. Within the hour Nehemiah appeared. His uncle was barely visible beneath the grime. His beard was matted, and his back bent with fatigue.

"You are to stay in bed, Bani," he said sternly.

It must have been a dream, Bani decided; that kiss, that whisper, he had dreamed them.

"I am all well," he protested, "and there is work to be done."

"So much work, Bani, that I have no time for you. I must get back. No one leaves his post any more."

Bani threw his cover off angrily. He was half out of bed when Nehemiah grasped him. "You have been very sick, Bani. I almost lost you." The boy saw the fear, no, the horror in Nehemiah's eyes, as he was pushed back against his pillow. "Stay here until Jadon gives you leave, Bani. Let me not be called again."

Bani lay back happily. He was weak. He realized it as soon as he tried to get up. But it had not been a dream. He knew. Now, no matter what happened, he knew. His uncle loved him. Perhaps, who knew, loved him as much as Jerusalem.

10

When he did get up, the walls were almost finished. **The** gates, of course, were not set in. But the cost had been heavy. For all these weeks no man had left the wall.

Like a shifting shadow, the enemy lurked; felt, but not seen. To be ready against it, Nehemiah commanded each who worked with trowel or shovel to wear a sword girded on his hip. As for those who bore away the rubbish in baskets upon their heads, they carried javelins in one hand, using the other to support their burdens.

The armed men wore coats of mail, and carried spears, shields and bows. While half stood ready, half labored. Behind each group, a Commander waited, should action be required.

In addition Nehemiah kept a trumpeter at his side constantly. "The work is great and large," he explained, "and we are separated upon the wall, one far from another. In whatever place you hear the sound of the horn, gather yourselves quickly unto us; and God will fight for us."

Night and day he kept Jerusalem under guard. None, he commanded, might leave the city. Only a few of the nobles grumbled. But even these dared not disobey.

Six weeks after that assembly on the Broad Place, the breaches were filled. Solid, the walls of Jerusalem stood; two hundred feet high.

The spaces gates should have filled were still empty. Yet as the last stone was laid, the people shouted with all their remaining strength. Upon each upraised head, from Ezra unto the youngest child, awe and joy mingled.

"Blessed are You, O Lord God," Ezra's voice rang out, "Who has permitted me to see this day."

"Amen!" Like a triumphal chorus, the answer swelled from each Jewish throat. There were tears, Bani saw, in the Scribe's eyes. There were tears in everyone's eyes. Even his own were wet.

But not Nehemiah's. Unmoved his rested upon the gateless spaces.

"TEKIAH!" It came from the other side of the wall. Each head turned towards its direction. Between the space of the northern gate a horseman appeared.

He carried no weapon; a fact he revealed by raising his arms over his shoulders. Then, cupping his hands, he shouted, "I bear a message from the Governor of Samaria. May I speak?"

"Speak!" Nehemiah signalled.

"My master, Sanballat," the man shouted, "and my lord, Geshem, of Arabia, ask for a meeting with the Governor of Judah, in one of the villages of the plain of Ono."

"Which one?"

"Whichever one your excellency shall choose."

Nehemiah's eyes did not so much as flicker. Gravely he said, "I am doing important work. You can see for yourself. The walls are done. But," he paused, "the gates are not set. I cannot come down."

"But," the messenger protested, "it is only twenty miles to Ono. A matter of a few days. My master begs you to spare him so short a time."

Nehemiah waved to the listening Judeans. "Let them decide," he said. And aloud, he cried, "My brothers, can the work cease? Can we stop now while yet the gates are not set?"

Exhausted, unwashed, the Judeans stared at him. Now that the walls were completed, they longed for a respite, for a change of clothes, a bath. But most of all, for their beds. Yet here was Nehemiah demanding that they go on. And here was this Samaritan urging Nehemiah to leave.

As swiftly as they had laid stone upon stone, so now, their minds laid fact upon fact: their enemies, having failed in all else, were now using honeyed words to conquer Jerusalem. Twenty miles was a distance; the enemy could overpower and assassinate Nehemiah.

Nehemiah! Their tower of strength! Until he had come all had despaired in the midst of ruins. Now, behold their resurrected walls, their resurrected hopes. A new blood coursed through their veins.

"No," cried the people. "The gates must first be set."

Nehemiah smiled. "Shall the work cease while I leave it and go down to parley?" he shouted. "Tell your masters we will first set the gates. Then, if they still desire, we will perhaps speak together."

The messenger hesitated, saluted, and galloped away.

Nehemiah's words rang out over the fading hoof beats. "There is no time to lose. They will never give up as long as Jerusalem is not completely protected. To the gates, my brothers!"

■ 141 ■

And as Nehemiah predicted, so it came to pass. Four more times the messenger returned, each time with the same request. And each time Nehemiah, replied, "There are still five gates left to be set"—or four, or three.

With the completion of each gate, some of the builders were dismissed.

During the whole of the next week no messenger came. Calm settled over the city. Only the Tekoites were working at the one remaining gate. Even Nehemiah, overcome with weariness, had to hand over the supervision to Hanani. Moreover, the political affairs of Judah now demanded his whole attention.

Bathed and combed, although still in simple robes, Nehemiah held court each day in his Hall of Audience. For the hungry of Jerusalem, as well as for the Jews who came from outside the city and for visiting dignitaries, Nehemiah maintained open house. Each day he fed more than one hundred and fifty men.

Tribute poured in, as it must, in all the lands of Artaxerxes. But the news spread rapidly: Nehemiah accepted taxes for the King's treasury, but not a shekel did he retain for himself.

Most of the wealthy of Judah refused to believe it. "A likely state of affairs," they sneered.

Bani rode freely about, heard their disbelief, and raged. His hand would fly to his sword, fingering its hilt. But then, it would drop helplessly.

Among the poor, opinion was divided. One morning Bani came upon a group whose patched tunics barely covered their nakedness.

"I tell you, a governor who refuses tribute is as possible as the Jordan flowing backward," Bani heard one of them declare.

"But Nehemiah fed us at the wall," someone objected.

"And worked as hard as any man," a third added.

"He's still a governor," the first insisted. "He must therefore be greedy."

"What about the scrolls and tablets he brought us?" a fourth suggested. "Ezra and all his scribes are busier than ever. I heard there are to be more schools throughout Judah. Our children will not grow up ignorant."

"Children! Whose children?" a woman in black demanded. "My son and daughter are sold into slavery. And yours. . . . How many of your daughters are already servants, how many of your sons are already on the way to the slave market?"

The bleeding face of Mazares the farmer flashed across Bani's memory. No, surely things like that did not happen here in Jerusalem.

But the woman had spied him. "There," her finger seemed to pierce his flesh, "is Nehemiah's son. He is safe. Like the sons of all the rich."

"I am his nephew," Bani muttered. Then beneath the silent but now hostile examination of the group, he said defiantly, "Why do you complain to each other?"

"To whom should we speak?" a man with a harelip asked. "To Meshullam?"

"To Nehemiah," the boy said curtly. "He is your governor."

"Even if he would, how can he redeem our sons?" the man asked. "He is wealthy, but not that wealthy."

Bani's lips curled. They did not know the sons of Hacaliah. "He will redeem Zion with justice," he said, unaware of how he repeated Nehemiah.

"What justice have the poor ever had?" the woman in black cried.

"In Jerusalem they must have justice," Bani said emphatically. Suddenly the words of Amos burned his lips.

"Justice shall well up as waters, righteousness as a mighty stream," he quoted. How clear it was now. Of course Jerusalem would have justice. Nehemiah had promised it in the evil city of Babylon. "Go to the palace," he commanded, "my uncle is holding court now."

"Listen to the pup," someone laughed. "He thinks he is Amos and Nehemiah together."

Hot tears blurred Bani's sight. What was the use? No matter what one said, or did, one was not believed. People had no faith.

He started. Had he faith? Was he any better than they?

"I am only his nephew," he said, managing with an effort to speak with restraint, "but I know my uncle. He will help you."

"Can he change the leopard's spots?" the woman jeered. "Can he teach charity to the rich?"

"He can judge justly." Bani said quietly. "If you let him. Go to him . . . he will listen."

"The boy is right," the harelip said. "How shall we receive justice, if we do not demand it? Let us go to Nehemiah.

But when they entered the Hall of Audience these men and women were struck dumb. Bani had to push the black-robed woman before his uncle.

"Is it you, Bani, or this woman, who has a petition?" Nehemiah asked.

"Judah, my lord."

"Then let Judeans speak. Come," he spoke kindly to the frightened woman, "tell me your grievance."

"There has been a famine in the land, my lord," the woman began.

"Yes," Nehemiah nodded encouragingly.

"We have had to get corn," she half pleaded. "We had no choice, we, our children were starving."

"What did you do?" Nehemiah asked.

"We mortgaged our fields."

"All of you?" Nehemiah appealed to the others.

"I, my vineyard," one said.

"I, my house," a third added.

"And for the King's tribute," the harelip explained, "we had to borrow money from the rich."

"From those who have already added field unto field," someone cried.

"Is not our flesh like the flesh of our brothers?" The woman had gained courage. "Are not our children like their children?"

"We are all descended from our father Abraham." Nehemiah's brows arched forward.

"Yet we bring our sons into bondage, and our daughters to be servants."

The Governor flushed with anger. His hands fiercely clutched the arm-rests of his throne.

The woman gasped, paled, and fell back.

"No, you are not done," Nehemiah commanded. "Speak on!"

"What more can I say, my lord?" she whispered. "They have our fields and vineyards. They have all we owned. We are at their mercy."

"So Sanballat was right." Nehemiah ground his teeth. "Jerusalem is no better than Samaria."

Bani trembled. He had never expected such fury. It was his fault for bringing these people here.

"Go home," Nehemiah commanded them, "each one of you, go home. The walls of Jerusalem shall not enclose this evil much longer."

"My lord," the harelip confronted Nehemiah, "why are you angry with us?"

"With you!" the Governor exclaimed, and slammed

his fist against the armrest. "For being the victims of greed? No, it is not you who corrupt Jerusalem." Then, gently, he added, "Go home, my brothers. All shall be set right."

"But," the man persisted, "it is not so simple. We did mortgage our land. We sold our vineyards legally."

"You cannot sell what is not yours."

"Not ours!" Not only the harelip, but all gasped.

"Have you forgotten," Nehemiah said, "that the land of Israel is only entrusted to you? Neither you nor they own it. The land is God's. He created it. And He is not Baal or Marduk. He is God, the God of Justice. Now, go home."

Silently, they bowed and departed.

That very afternoon, Nehemiah met with the chief nobles and rulers. Without any warning, he accused them. "You lend upon pledge, every one of you to your brothers. Here in Jerusalem, upon this altar of God."

"We must take pledges," Meshullam said boldly. "We are not as rich as Nehemiah!"

"Then come to my table, and I shall feed you too."

Meshullam flushed. "I did not say I needed your bread."

"What do you need?" Nehemiah asked. "The cry of the poor, the weeping of children, the wailing of bereft mothers?"

"This is business!" Meshullam declared. "Not charity."

"This is Jerusalem, not Babylon! Tomorrow you and all who own a pledge shall meet with me. In the Broad Place before the Water Gate." Curtly, "I bid you good day."

Sullenly they left the Hall of Audience.

They came the next day as he had commanded. Flanked again by Ezra and Eliashib, Nehemiah stood before them on the dais. Again he plunged into the heart of the evil.

"According to our ability, we have redeemed our brothers, the Jews, that sold themselves into bondage. Now, would you sell your brothers, and should they sell themselves unto us?" He paused, but no one, not even Meshullam, responded. "The thing that you do is not good," he continued. "Ought you not to walk in the fear of God, because of the reproach of the heathen our enemies? Or wherein are we sons of the Covenant?"

He surveyed the crowd expectantly. No man made a sound. They were stiff, waiting. But for what? Bani wondered.

With a softer tongue Nehemiah went on. "I, likewise, my brothers, and my servants too have lent money and corn." Bani started. To what kind of guilt was Nehemiah confessing? "I pray you," Nehemiah pleaded, "let us leave off this exaction."

A breath of relief seemed to rise from these men. Spines curved, weights shifted, leaning more comfortably on gold-crested canes. Some lips even smiled.

But Bani was angry. Nehemiah had saved their pride, by making himself one of them. But he was not one of them. No, nor ever could be.

"Restore, I pray you, to them," Nehemiah raised his hands, "even this very day, their fields, their vineyards, their oliveyards, and their houses; also the hundreds of pieces of silver, and the corn, the wine, and the oil that you exact of them."

Hassaneah stepped forward. "I will restore them," he said, "and I will require nothing of them; so will I do, even as you say." And turning to the others he cried, "What do you say, my brothers?"

With a great shout they replied, "We will make restoration, and will require nothing of them; we will do as Nehemiah advises."

"Eliashib," Nehemiah said to the High Priest, "they have spoken well. Administer the oath, that they shall act according to their promise."

"What?" Meshullam cried indignantly. "Is not our word sufficient for Nehemiah? Must we swear to it?"

Nehemiah, who but a minute before had been one of them, was suddenly the Cupbearer of Artaxerxes. As one inspects an ugly insect, Nehemiah examined Meshullam.

Meshullam, however, was not daunted. "I," he cried, "shall take no oath! Nor shall I relinquish my mortgages. They are legally mine."

Before anyone knew what had happend, Nehemiah was off the dais, had seized Meshullam by his beard and flung him to the ground, and had spat over the prostrate body. "Shall a man who has already given his daughter unto Tobiah's son continue to profane Jerusalem? You shall return your pledges, Meshullam. Or I shall teach you God's law more painfully."

And as Meshullam struggled to his feet, Nehemiah again spoke commandingly from the dais. "Administer the oath, High Priest."

Eliashib obeyed. All answered, "Amen."

Then Nehemiah shook out his robe and said, "So God shake out every man from his house and from his fields if he does not perform this promise. Even so let him be shaken out and emptied."

"Amen," again they replied.

"Go in peace, my brothers," Nehemiah said.

"Shalom," they replied and left the Broad Place.

But as they left, Bani knew that fresh enemies had been

created against the House of Hacaliah that day. Still, justice had been done.

He peered into the Temple through the Water Gate. The afternoon service was over. The fire burned upon the altar. Was it his imagination, or was its flame purer? Suddenly he wanted to kneel upon the stone, to thank God he was a Jew. But his back remained straight. It would not do to make a spectacle of himself.

Next day the messenger of Sanballat returned, this time with a letter.

"Read it," Nehemiah said to Bani, almost indifferently, handing it over.

"It is reported among the nations," the boy began, "and Geshem says it too, that you and the Jews think to rebel. For that reason you built walls. It is also reported that you are ambitious to be king."

Bani's mouth was suddenly dry.

"Read on, Bani!"

He swallowed hard, held the parchment closer, struggled to steady his voice.

"And you have also appointed prophets," he read, "to proclaim you at Jerusalem saying, Here is a king in Judah. And now it shall be reported to the King according to these words."

The boy could hardly see. A throbbing in his head blurred his vision.

"Is that all, Bani?"

"Just this sentence, my lord. 'Come now, and let us take council together.' Signed, Sanballat."

"Let me have it Bani."

His eyes blurred with tears, he handed back the letter. He heard rather than saw the parchment crumpled and torn.

"Tell your master," Nehemiah said to the messenger, "there are no such things done as he says, that he has woven a useless web of falsehoods."

As the man turned he came face to face with Hanani, who had just entered. Nehemiah's cousin brought joyful news.

"It is done, Nehemiah! The gate is set."

"Ah, just in time." Nehemiah stood up and called the messenger back. "Wait. I have another word for Sanballat. Tell him Jerusalem is safe—from him and all her enemies. Here, on this twenty-fifth day of Elul, fifty-two days after we began, God has enabled us to restore His fortress and His Sanctuary. Now go!"

But Bani felt no joy. One image, and one alone confronted him.

"What is it, Bani?" Nehemiah was studying him curiously.

"Nothing . . . nothing."

"You are trembling, Bani."

"It is just . . . just . . ."

"Yes?"

"The Makrian, my lord!" he burst out. "I can't help remembering him."

"What has the Makrian to do with you or me?"

"He rebuilt the walls of his city."

"So . . . ?"

"And was accused of treason. As you will be, by Sanballat."

"For fulfilling Artaxerxes' command?"

"But they say you want to be a king?"

"And do I?"

"Of course not."

"Then what do you fear?"

"That Artaxerxes might believe them."

Nehemiah smiled. "If we tremble before the threats of wicked men, we shall never achieve anything. Forget them. This is but their desperation talking." He paused. "We shall not be frightened, shall we, my son."

"No." Bani glowed. It was good to be called son, by Nehemiah. "No!" he said more forcefully. "And besides," he was struck by a new idea, "what prophet will ever say you hired him?"

"False ones, Bani," Nehemiah said grimly, "we have always had these too."

"Who would believe false prophets?"

"Whoever wants to." And as Bani paled, Nehemiah said sharply, "What? Do you still tremble for these evil men . . . or women? Are you a son of Hacaliah, or a slave . . . ?"

"A son of Hacaliah," Bani said stiffly.

"And therefore, my son," Nehemiah added gently, "have faith. Believe that this evil scheme must fail. This is what it means to believe in God."

"Hanani," Nehemiah said, turning to his cousin, "you and Hananiah must take over the security of Jerusalem."

"Yes, Nehemiah."

"Let not the gates be opened until the sun be hot; and while they stand on guard, let them shut the doors, and bar them; and let watches be appointed among the inhabitants of Jerusalem, every one in his watch, and let every one set a watch on his own house."

"There are so few in Jerusalem," Hanani frowned, "now that the builders have left."

"Then we shall have to bring in more."

"But there are no houses for them. How shall they live?"

"If need be, Hanani, I shall build for them."

A pause and Hanani said, "Nehemiah, I cannot forget how I tried to prevent you from coming to Jerusalem. At night especially, it haunts me."

"Haunts you?" Nehemiah smiled.

"I think how I might have stopped you." He covered his eyes as one who would black out a dream. "But what would we, Jerusalem, have done without you?"

"I am God's servant, Hanani. If He had not chosen me, He would have chosen another. Neither you nor I can change Israel's destiny."

For a moment Hanani did not move. Then, bowing before Nehemiah, he said, "But He did choose you. Blessed are you, Nehemiah, among Israel."

"Blessed be Israel, Hanani," Nehemiah replied, "His nation of messengers among the nations."

11

Within the next few days Jerusalem was moved by a new
spirit. The sacred month of Tishri was approaching, and
the people reminded themselves that the first day was a
solemn day of rest, a memorial proclaimed by a trumpet
blast, a holy convocation. "You shall do no manner of
work," many recalled, "and you shall bring an offering of
fire unto God."

They were like men who have journeyed across wide
deserts, and who, when at last safely arrived at their destination, realize how weary they were and how thirsty.

Without being summoned, the people gathered together and assembled in the Broad Place, and spoke unto
Ezra the Scribe, desiring him to bring the book of the Law
of Moses, which the Lord had commanded to Israel.

And Ezra, who was also a priest, brought the Law before the congregation of men and women upon the first
day of the seventh month. And he stood upon a pulpit
of wood, which they had made for the purpose. On his
right hand and on his left stood Levites. And Ezra un-

rolled the scroll in the sight of all the people, and when he opened it all the people stood to attention.

And Ezra blessed the Lord. And all the people answered Amen, Amen, with a raising of hands. And they bowed their heads, and fell down before the Lord with their faces to the ground.

But Ezra made them stand before he began to read. From early morning until midday, he read, waiting for the Levites to interpret each sentence distinctly.

And as the people understood God's word, they realized they had not fulfilled His commandments. Therefore they wept for their sins and for their ignorance that had brought them to sin.

But Ezra comforted them. "This day is holy unto the Lord our God. Therefore mourn not, nor weep, but go your way, eat fat, and drink sweet wine, and send portions unto them for whom nothing is prepared. For this day is holy unto our Lord. Therefore, be not grieved, for the Lord is our joy and strength."

So the people rejoiced that day in their Torah, sending portions to the needy.

On the next day, the second day of Tishri, they gathered themselves again before Ezra in the Broad Place. And this time they found written in the Law how the Lord had commanded them to dwell in booths in the feast of the seventh month.

For the next thirteen days the people of Judah went forth and fetched olive branches, and branches of wild olive, and myrtle branches and palm branches and branches of thick trees, and made themselves booths upon the roofs of their houses, and in their courts, and in the courts of the Temple, and in the Broad Place of the Water Gate, and in the Broad Place of the Gate of Ephraim.

This time the people rejoiced with greater gladness. Beneath their flimsy boughs they were Israel again, all equally dependent upon God, as they had been in the time of their wanderings.

For seven days Ezra read to them and instructed them. On the eighth day, the twenty-second day of Tishri, there was a solemn assembly according to the Law.

The festival season should have been over. But the people were not satisfied. They had rejoiced. But they had not atoned. They had not made peace with God for the years before Nehemiah had come.

Two days later, therefore, on the twenty-fourth day of Tishri, the children of Israel again assembled. They covered their heads with ashes, their limbs with sackcloth; nor would they eat or drink. All who were gathered separated themselves from all foreigners, standing and confessing their sins and the sins of their fathers.

For six hours the Levites read to them in the Torah, and for six hours the people knelt and prayed. Then a certain number of the Levites cried, "Come, arise and bless the Lord your God from everlasting to everlasting."

And the people stood up, raised their hands to heaven and replied, "Blessed be His glorious Name that is exalted above all blessing and praise."

Evening shadows striped the Temple stones. A cold pure wind blew and freshened every cheek. It was almost dark when the Levites stepped down from the pulpit, and silence fell upon the assembly like a holy veil.

Then, barefoot and in sackcloth and ashes, Nehemiah climbed to the empty pulpit. And as he faced Israel, he seemed to be looking into each man's heart. Yet when he spoke, it was not to the assembly, but to the God of Israel.

"You are the Lord," he began, "even You alone; You

have made heaven, the heaven of heavens with their host, the earth and all things on it, the seas and all that is in them and You preserve them all . . ."

Like the Torah, Nehemiah began with creation. Yet no one stirred. So close was each to Nehemiah, he would have listened if it took the whole night.

"You," Nehemiah continued, "chose Abram . . . out of Ur of the Chaldees . . . made a Covenant with him . . . saw our affliction in Egypt . . . came down also upon Mount Sinai . . . gave right judgments and laws of truth . . . bread from heaven for their hunger . . ."

On and on Nehemiah went, reviewing their history, their glories and their failures. Gradually he forged the chain; shaping their first link from the mysteries of creation, and their other links of all that had happened to them, both good and evil. He spared nothing, and no one. Neither kings nor priests, neither princes nor Israelites. All were guilty, but all were still Israel.

They had received the Covenant. They had broken the Covenant. Now they must renew the Covenant.

". . . a sure Covenant," he said sternly, "and subscribe it; and our princes and our Levites and our priests shall set their seal unto it."

He unrolled a scroll and read the document he and Ezra had drawn up. There was nothing new in it. But those laws which were essential for the survival of this tiny community of Judah were written out clearly and simply.

When Nehemiah finished, he raised his seal on high.

"Behold," he said, "I, Nehemiah, the Governor, the son of Hacaliah affix my seal to this Covenant. Let all the leaders of Israel who would sign set their seal upon it too."

And so in the growing darkness, before the people, the heads of twenty-one priestly houses, of seventeen levitical houses, and of forty-four of the chief families of Israel, affixed their seals to the Renewed Covenant.

When Baanah, the last of the Elders, had finished, Nehemiah called upon Ezra to read from the book of Exodus.

And Ezra read, "Now if you will hearken to My voice indeed, and keep my Covenant, then you shall be mine own treasure from among all peoples; for all the earth is Mine; and you shall be unto Me a kingdom of priests and a holy nation."

With all Israel, Bani answered, "All that the Lord has spoken we shall do."

12

With the renewal of the Covenant, Jerusalem was renewed. Her walls shone by day, and glimmered by night. Houses were scrubbed and repaired, streets were levelled and repaved. Within the Temple between services clanged the tools of Levites who were masons and carpenters.

On Shabbat all activity ceased. Except for footsteps climbing the Temple Mount, or the song of a thrush, Jerusalem was still.

It had not been difficult to teach the beauty and holiness of Shabbat, after the signing of the Renewed Covenant. No one treaded grapes in his winepress on Shabbat, nor brought in heaps of corn upon his donkey, no, nor wines, nor grapes, nor figs, nor any manner of victuals or supplies. Even the Syrians, those strangers within the gates, refrained from selling their fish on Shabbat.

One nobleman, it is true, did order his grapes pressed on Shabbat.

"But they are my grapes," he insisted before Nehemiah.

"And if there be a sin, then it shall be my sin, and my risk."

"Shall it be?" said Nehemiah. "Did not your fathers do this, and did not our God therefore bring all this evil upon us and upon this city? Would you bring more wrath upon Israel by profaning Shabbat?"

The nobleman paled. But whether he feared Nehemiah's anger, or God's, Bani could not decide.

For most of Judah, however, it was neither one nor the other. Shabbat was kept with joy and love, as indeed were all of God's laws.

When Nehemiah took a census, and called upon the people to draw lots, they responded happily. The tenth who were chosen to dwell in Jerusalem, went willingly . . . The others sent them on their way with gifts and blessings. True to his word, Nehemiah built homes for the new arrivals.

During the month of Heshban, Nehemiah hardly left his Hall of Audience except to study plans and confer with Eliashib and Ezra.

When he called upon Israel to support the Temple, gifts poured in lavishly. Twenty thousand darics of gold, two thousand pounds of silver, and sixty-seven priestly tunics were the offerings of the Judeans. The elders who had signed the Covenant, sent separate gifts: twenty thousand darics of gold and twenty-two thousand pounds of silver. Nehemiah presented one thousand darics of gold, fifty basins, and five hundred and thirty priestly tunics.

With Ezra, Nehemiah established schools. Each week of Heshban, as well as at the beginning of Kielev, disciples of Ezra left Jerusalem, their carts piled with precious scrolls. All this time, neither messenger nor sword descended from Samaria.

If only they could live in peace, Bani prayed. Jerusalem

was so beautiful. He could hardly describe her special grace. Unless it was the golden glow of her stars singing so low; or the brilliance of her moon upon her hills; or the purity of her dawns, bathed in their heavenly dew.

To awaken each morning beneath her pearl-grey veil, the morning star trembling, the sweet scent of a reborn world so clean it fairly ached in his nostrils, was Jerusalem. To lift up his eyes to her mountains, Zion, Olives, Tzofim, swelling away from the Temple Mount of Moriah, soft waves of green and rock, wings of Moriah itself, was also Jerusalem. But most of all to walk where his fathers had walked, where Isaiah had preached, Jeremiah had wept, David had sung, where all the hosts of men and women whose blood ran in his veins had engraved tears, laughter and prayers into her stone, this was his Jerusalem.

And when Nehemiah decided to celebrate her rebirth with the dedication of her walls, Bani agreed with all his heart. As he galloped throughout Judah announcing the glad tidings, he knew Israel shared his joy. To the Levites who were musicians and to those who were singers he flew. Across the Plains of the Jordan, to the villages of Netophah and Beth Gilgal, and the fields of Geba and Azmaveth.

Within Jerusalem preparations began immediately. The priests and Levites purified themselves, the people, the Gates, and the wall. And each day, as more Judeans arrived, they purified them as well.

In the Temple the loaves of thanksgiving were baked. The musicians polished trumpets, cymbals, psalteries, and all the other instruments King David had devised. The choirmaster held rehearsal after rehearsal.

The supervisor of the priestly garments fussed over each tunic.

Even the Tekoites, who came from their little village, had combed their beards.

In honor of the great day, Nehemiah had invited all heads of families to dinner on the preceding evening.

On the evening of the twenty-fourth of Kislev, Nehemiah, Governor of Judah, presided at the head of his banquet board. On his right side sat Ezra, on his left, Eliashib.

Huge candelabras, burning oil, threw uneven light upon the festivity. This was not the Apadana, Bani thought, but it was grand and colorful. Gold pendants, silver rings, purple and blue wools, velvety crimsons, and the multi-colored beards, white, black, red, grey and brown, blended into a living tapestry, warm and throbbing.

Whatever differences had separated these elders before, were laid aside this evening. Eliashib, Meshullam, even he who had pressed grapes on Shabbat, rubbed shoulders with Hanani, Ezra and Shallum. And at the head of all, Nehemiah reigned, completely relaxed. Yet no one spoke to him unless addressed first.

A choir was about to perform. Jezrahiah, their leader, raised his hand. All conversation ceased. But before the hands descended the horn shrilled.

TEKIAH!

No one stirred.

TEKIAH!

Nehemiah sat up. There was no mistaking this second blast.

Footsteps, martial, purposeful, neared the banquet. All eyes centered upon the doorway.

A man appeared in its frame. The resplendent uniform of a Persian General draped over his shoulders. Bani's heart leaped. Yes, it was he . . .

"Oebazus!" Nehemiah was out of his chair. Pure joy

illuminated his face. "Oebazus!" He started towards him, stopped suddenly.

The joy faded. His brows were a straight line of disbelief.

Behind Oebazus Sanballat hovered . . . and at his side, Tobiah, and yet a third . . . one with ice blue eyes . . . and Bani stared, no red jewel between them.

"My lord," Nehemiah said coldly. "Welcome to Jerusalem."

Oebazus bowed. He offered neither hand for clasping, nor shoulder for embracing.

Instead he unrolled a scroll. "I come from Artaxerxes, King of Kings."

Bani frowned. How that title, so natural in Susa, offended him in Jerusalem.

"And what is His Majesty's pleasure?" Nehemiah asked stiffly.

"To answer the charge of treason brought by the Governors of Samaria, Ammon, and Arabia." Oebazus advanced into the banquet hall.

"Unto whom?" Nehemiah asked sharply.

"To His Majesty's representative."

Bani felt as if a cold cord was being wound about his throat. So it had come to this! What he had feared for so long was now a fact. The bleeding face of the Makrian swam before him.

"Who is His Majesty's representative?"

"I am."

At first Bani could have wept for relief, for surely Oebazus would never harm Nehemiah. But then he remembered. Oebazus' father had been executed, his skin flayed, tanned and stretched to cushion a chair for his son. . . .

Bani shuddered. How could one judge the hearts of men, how depend on them? Artaxerxes was just, even kind at times. . . . But to make Oebazus the judge of his friend was cruel . . . as cruel as the torture of the Makrian.

He looked towards Nehemiah. The candelabras smoked, casting a black pall over him. . . . Before all, the Governor of Judah darkened. Bani searched the guests. They were tense. With fear, Bani knew. Except perhaps Meshullum. Was he wrong or was the man communicating with Tobiah? He studied him, and as though aware of this scrutiny, Meshullam averted his face.

"Let the representative of His Majesty take the seat due him." Nehemiah pointed to his own chair.

Without a protest, Oebazus sat down. "My lords," he said to the three governors who had accompanied him, "stand here, at my right. Now, Nehemiah, these are your accusers. What do you say?"

"I say they are liars!"

Was that a smile flickering on the face of Oebazus? No, Bani decided, he must have been mistaken. But the three governors had reddened, and their hands grasped the hilts of their swords.

"My lords," Oebazus said sharply, "this is a court of Persian law. Proof, not swords!"

"They have rebuilt the walls of Jerusalem," said Sanballat at last.

"As His Majesty ordered," Nehemiah said. "Shall I send for a copy of His Majesty's letter from the Satrap, Adeus?"

"I have seen the letter," Oebazus said. "The King ordered it." And to the three he added, "That is no proof."

"He does not fulfill the law of Persia," Tobiah said.

"How so?" Oebazus demanded.

"He does not collect the taxes."

Oebazus' eyebrows lifted. He turned to Nehemiah.

"All of His Majesty's taxes have been sent to Adeus,"

Nehemiah spoke coolly, as though Tobiah were not in his presence.

"It is not true, ask Mesh . . ." Tobiah began, then caught himself.

"Meshullam!" Nehemiah swerved towards the man.

Meshullam crouched against his chair, paralyzed with fear.

"Stand up!" Nehemiah commanded. And as the man shrank farther, Nehemiah hauled him to his feet and shoved him before Oebazus. "Speak! Have I or have I not collected the King's taxes?"

"A half. . . ." Meshullam managed to gasp.

The elders of Israel, even Eliashib, showed their dismay.

"Whose half?" Nehemiah prodded Meshullam, and as the man collapsed, he cast him away in disgust. "High Priest," Nehemiah said, "speak to the representative of His Majesty, tell him what portion I have collected."

"The Governor of Judah has collected the taxes due His Majesty, Artaxerxes," said Eliashib, clearly, springing to his feet.

"And what of your portion, Nehemiah, the half due all His Majesty's Satraps?" Oebazus asked.

"I have not, nor ever shall eat the bread of a Satrap," Nehemiah said proudly.

"But it is your due," Oebazus said with a touch of awe.

"To lay burdens upon my brothers, to take their bread and wine—never, my lord."

"But the former governors, who were also Jews, did so."

"They had no other means. I," Nehemiah looked squarely at Oebazus, "have, by the grace of God, more than my share."

Sanballat, Tobiah, and Geshem were bent forward as though better to see this man, Nehemiah. A pause, and Oebazus leaned back against his chair, tapped upon its arms, and asked briskly:

"Well, my lords, is this all your proof?"

For the minute they were mute as stupid students before a difficult problem. "I said, is that all?" Oebazus snapped.

"No!" Geshem recovered. "He," and his finger pointed at Nehemiah, "he wants to be king."

Oebazus eyed the Arabian sharply. "Be careful, Geshem."

"It is true," Geshem insisted. "He has made a new pact with his people." And as Nehemiah frowned, he cried triumphantly, "He thought we did not know. But we know everything. Make him produce it, Oebazus. Make him. You will see his seal upon it, yes, and the seals of most of these traitorous men."

"Is this true, Nehemiah?" Oebazus asked.

"In part, my lord."

Oebazus paled. Bani's heart beat like a hammer. Oebazus did love Nehemiah. He knew it. But what anguish for the Persian! For he would be as ruthless with Nehemiah as with Sanballat, if need be. No one knew better than Oebazus what Artaxerxes demanded of his judges.

"Which part?" Oebazus asked.

"I have drawn up a Covenant. Or rather renewed our old Covenant.

"What covenant?"

"The Covenant of our God."

"Clumsy lies," Sanballat jeered. "What need would there be for such a covenant if it were the same as their old? Any fool would see through that."

"I would not expect understanding from one who thinks

■ 168 ■

he can worship the God of Israel while kneeling to Baal,"
Nehemiah said with contempt. "The Covenant of Israel
and God, is a covenant of all eternity. God who is perfect
keeps His part, but we who are imperfect, have broken
our part. It is necessary for him who breaks to mend,
Oebazus. It is necessary for him who breaks his vow to
renew it."

"By their own admission, Israel is a nation of liars,"
Sanballat mocked. "And this is the Israel that thinks her-
self so specially favored that she will not allow anyone
else to enter her fold. I tell you, as Israel has been untrue to her God, so Israel is untrue to Artaxerxes."

Bani swallowed hard. The Ammonite, at the first assembly, had mocked at Israel, and Nehemiah had merely
smiled—as he was smiling now. At the first assembly,
Nehemiah had refused to answer the Ammonite. Would
he refuse now?

"There are two charges here, Nehemiah," Oebazus said
firmly, "disloyalty to your God; and disloyalty to Artaxerxes. You must answer both."

Bani hardly dared breathe. Not only Oebazus, but he
himself wanted an explanation. If Israel sinned, why indeed was she so special?

"Well," Oebazus said. "We are waiting."

Nehemiah folded his arms across his chest. "As you
say," he bowed. And looking straight into the Persian's
eyes, he said, "As for disloyalty to Artaxerxes, I shall not
argue what is beneath me. My yes has always meant
yes; my no, no. I have sworn loyalty to the King. I never
have, nor ever shall, be false to my word.

"But as regards disloyalty to God and our Renewed
Covenant, you must, in order to understand these matters,
understand the very meaning of the name, Israel. Israel
means 'one who struggles with God.' Our father Jacob

■ 169 ■

was named Israel only after he had wrestled with God's messenger. For it is our destiny to struggle. And, as in all struggles, we sometimes conquer. Then, indeed, like our father, Jacob, we are Israel. Sometimes, alas, we are defeated. But triumphant or defeated, we must go on with the battle. That is why we renewed our Covenant, to give us strength for the battle before us."

"Against these men?" Oebazus nodded at the three governors.

"Against . . ." Nehemiah broke off and stepped back as though any contact with his three accusers would contaminate him. The three men shuddered, then flushed.

"Against whom, or what?" Oebazus prodded.

"Against ourselves. Against the evil impulses we all have."

"You see!" Sanballat crowed. "He admits it."

Again that smile of disdain curved Nehemiah's lips. And again he ignored the Samaritan. "Does Oebazus know of any man free of them?" he asked. And as Oebazus nodded thoughtfully, Nehemiah continued, "We must struggle constantly if we are to keep God's commandments. You have studied Jewish law, and therefore know it is not easy to live according to our Torah."

"Make him show you the Covenant," Geshem cried, "you will see the treason he has planned."

Oebazus did not answer. Then, as though it were his own idea, he said, "Produce the Covenant, Nehemiah."

"It is in the Temple, Oebazus."

"Let it be brought."

Obediently, Jadon left and in a short while returned with the scroll. Bowing, he handed it to Oebazus. The Persian unrolled it, inspected its signatures.

"Read!" he commanded Jadon.

In the tense silence Jadon obeyed.

"We the children of Israel do enter into covenant to walk in God's law, which was given by Moses the servant of God; to observe and do all the commandments of the Lord our God and to keep His ordinances and His statutes." He paused. Oebazus nodded.

"We," Jadon continued, "shall not give our daughters unto the people of the land, nor take their daughters for our sons; and if the people of the land bring ware or any victual on Shabbat to sell, we will not buy of them on the Shabbat or on any holy day."

Again Oebazus nodded, and again Jadon read on.

"We shall forego the seventh year, allowing the land to lie fallow. What the land produces of itself shall be for us, for the poor, for the strangers, and for the cattle and for the beasts.

"Also we shall forego on the seventh year what is owed to us. That which we have lent our neighbor shall we release, because the Lord has proclaimed a release every seventh year."

Jadon paused. Gently Oebazus said, "Is that all, Master Jadon?"

"That is all except for the rules concerning the Temple. Let my lord read these if he chooses." Jadon offered him the scroll.

Oebazus' eyes scanned the parchment. He raised them at last, and held the scroll with its imprint of eighty-two seals before the three accusers. "Does this satisfy you?" he asked.

The three were stunned. They looked frantically at each other, at Oebazus, and again at the document.

"Well," Oebazus said icily. "Are you suddenly speechless?"

"It is a forgery," Geshem burst out desperately, "it is not the original document. Search their Temple. You will find the other."

Bani could not contain himself any longer. "Shall he who tried to murder the Governor of Judah," he cried, "dare to accuse him? Oebazus, Geshem is an assassin."

Oebazus' expression was as hard as granite. "You are no longer an irresponsible boy, Bani. This is a court of justice," he said. "Keep it well in mind!"

"Justice is what I seek," said Bani as he stepped forward, without looking either at Nehemiah or Jadon. "What justice can we have," he asked, "when men who delight in killing become our accusers? I repeat, Geshem of Arabia tried to lure Nehemiah into an ambush to kill him."

Oebazus turned to Geshem. "What do you say?"

"The boy is mad."

"I saw him, Oebazus, in Susa. You too saw him then."

"I!" Oebazus frowned. "I do not recall it."

"You didn't notice him. But he was in the Corridor." And as Oebazus continued to frown, he cried, "But he was there, as he was at his campfire, and at the attack before Charchemish."

"He is a liar too," Geshem laughed. "He is even trying to convince you of a lie. I have never seen him before in my life."

"*He* lies. I heard him outline the whole plot. Over his campfire."

"At night, Bani?" Oebazus asked.

"Yes, at night."

"But can you be sure of anyone in the dark, Bani?"

"It was he! Those eyes, the voice, only . . ." he faltered, "he wore a red jewel on his turban. He always wore a red jewel."

"I see none now, Bani," Oebazus said sternly.

"No . . . but at the attack others saw him."

"Nehemiah," Oebazus turned to the Governor of Judah, "would you swear upon your Torah you saw Geshem?"

Nehemiah paused. "I saw the jewel Bani saw; heard this voice . . . but below his eyes, his face was concealed. No, I cannot swear. Sure as I may be, I cannot swear."

"My uncle," Bani pleaded, "you know it was he!"

"I cannot swear it, Bani," Nehemiah said, shaking his head, "my oath is too sacred."

"You see," Geshem crowed, "even the boy's uncle will not support him."

"You have no other proof, Bani?" Oebazus asked.

Bani searched his mind furiously. Surely there was some way of proving the truth. The silence was profound. He knew there was evidence somewhere, if he could think clearly. . . .

Suddenly his heart leaped. Yes, it had to be.

"Oebazus," he breathed, "it is he. I know now. These men, all of them, attacked my uncle . . . they won't dare deny that. . . ."

"And we would again!" Sanballat said. "We are loyal to Artaxerxes. It is our duty to destroy treason against our King."

"But before Charchemish. Before we came to Jerusalem you could not know what Nehemiah planned. When Geshem tried to kill my uncle . . ."

"Oebazus," Geshem snapped, "this spawn of treason sneers at the dignity of our King's court. I have told you, I never saw him before, either at Charchemish or here. Never."

"Geshem is right," Oebazus said sternly, "you cannot accuse wildly, Bani. Your youth will not protect falsehood."

"Then, how, if I never saw him before, do I know what Geshem has under his tunic?"

Geshem laughed. Everyone knows what men wear . . .

"Upon his right shoulder. . . ." Bani continued.

Geshem's hands flew to his shoulder. His eyes were slits. Each man in the room might have become a statue.

"What is on his right shoulder, Bani?" Oebazus whispered.

"A scar!" Geshem's hand dropped. He stepped back. "Look at it, Oebazus, it is there . . . I know . . ." Unless, he trembled, unless that arrow had not penetrated to the flesh . . . sweat gathered under his armpit. It had to . . . He had drawn the bow way back. It just had to.

"Take off your robes," Oebazus commanded the Arab.

"He lies, I tell you." Geshem gathered his robe about him. "I was never there." He started for the door.

"Seize him!" Oebazus called.

The Arab lunged forward. But Sanballat and Tobiah, flashing a signal, grabbed him first. Instantly they disrobed him. Before all, upon the right shoulder, the mark of an arrow emerged, white after four months, yet plainly outlined. But clearer than the scar, was a red jewel, dangling upon his chest.

"True!" Sanballat exclaimed and pushing his ally at Oebazus' feet he added, "We are guiltless, Oebazus. Tobiah and I had not part in this."

"Dogs!" Geshem glared up at them furiously. "Cowards! Liars!"

"Silence!" Oebazus said. And in the hush, he asked, "Did you see Sanballat and Tobiah before Charchemish, Bani?"

"No, Oebazus." And Bani smiled, unaware that his disdainful smile was exactly like Nehemiah's.

"Then we have to accept their word." Sanballat and

Tobiah lowered their eyes to conceal their satisfaction. "For the while," Oebazus added. "But His Majesty will not be pleased. The Great King seeks the favor of the God of Israel. Be advised, you two. Keep the peace." He paused, "Now, leave us!"

They swung upon their heels, walking rapidly, but not running. They were not fast enough, however, to escape Oebazus' command. "Arrest Geshem. He shall learn what Persian justice is."

Once again the Makrian's face swam before Bani's memory. In spite of everything he could not bear to look on.

Oebazus was on his feet now. "This is your chair, Nehemiah he said. "I am no longer your judge."

"You were never my judge, Oebazus."

"No?" Oebazus tried to smile, but could not quite.

"Only God is my Judge."

"Then what was I?" Oebazus frowned.

Nehemiah smiled. "An honest man. And, I hope, my friend."

Before the astonished elders, Oebazus and Nehemiah embraced.

Strange, Bani thought, Oebazus was probably the only man who loved Nehemiah unreservedly. And he was not a Jew.

Next day, the twenty-fifth day of Kislev, two processions, one led by Ezra, and one by Nehemiah, circled the wall. Before each procession walked the priestly and Levitical musicians.

Thanksgiving offerings, gifts of a grateful people, with the loaves that accompanied them, were held high by the citizens of Judah.

How the companies sparkled! How purely the trained

voices pierced to the very heavens! And with what fervor the trumpeters blew, the harpists twanged, the cymbalists and drummers clanged and pounded.

Bani marched behind Nehemiah. And behind him came elders, rulers, men, even women and children.

Upon the wall they went, over the tower of the Furnaces, until the broad wall, then around to the Gate of Ephraim in the center of the north wall, past the Gate of the Old City, the Fish Gate, the Towers of Hananel and Hammeah, and as far as the Sheep Gate and the Gate of the Guard. Then, at last, they assembled on the familiar meeting place, the Broad Place at the east side of the Temple.

Here they met Ezra's procession. And here all the singers joined in the ecstatic Psalm of the musician King.

> Hallelujah.
> Praise God in His sanctuary;
> Praise Him in the firmament of His power.
>
> Praise Him for His mighty acts;
> Praise Him according to His abundant greatness.
>
> Praise Him with the blast of the horn;
> Praise Him with the psaltery and harp.
>
> Praise Him with the timbrel and dance;
> Praise Him with stringed instruments and the pipe.
>
> Praise Him with the loud-sounding cymbals;
> Praise Him with the clanging cymbals.
>
> Let everything that has breath praise the Lord.
> Hallelujah.

How good it was to be here, thought Bani, how good to be among one's people. He needed no mirror to know that his face radiated joy. That joy was reflected in the faces of all Israel on this Day of Dedication.

Later that evening, after the sacrifices and prayers, after the dancing and singing, Bani returned with his uncle to the Governor's House, where Oebazus was waiting for them.

"I am leaving, Nehemiah," he announced.

"So soon! But you have just come."

"I must report to Adeus at Sidon, then go back to Susa. Artaxerxes wants an immediate, and," he smiled wryly, "a personal report."

"So it is farewell."

"For a while, Nehemiah."

"A little more than eleven years, Oebazus."

"That much!" Oebazus paused. "It is a long time, Nehemiah, a long time." He held out both hands, one to Nehemiah and one to Bani. "If I am in Susa then, I shall welcome you both."

"So you shall, Oebazus," Nehemiah said.

"And you, Bani. Your lance with the golden pomegranate is waiting for you."

The boy stood very straight, at attention. "Give it to another," he said. "I shall not return to Susa."

"What!" Oebazus exclaimed. "What are you saying?"

"I shall never leave Jerusalem, Oebazus, not if I can help it."

"My promise to Artaxerxes, Bani," Nehemiah said. "Have you forgotten?"

"Yours, my uncle. Not mine."

"You would stay without me, Bani?" Nehemiah's eyes pierced his heart.

Bani paled. "Yes," he whispered.

"And I thought you loved your uncle, Bani." Oebazus said.

"I do!" Bani cried. "Oh, I do."

"But Jerusalem more. Is that it, Bani?" Oebazus persisted.

The boy considered a moment, examining his conscience. For years he had hated Jerusalem because he had believed it dearer to Nehemiah than himself. Now suddenly it was plain. Nehemiah's love for him, Nehemiah's love for Jerusalem; they could not be compared.

"It is not a matter of more, Oebazus." He spoke slowly. "I love Jerusalem. She is my home . . . But I love my uncle too. I cannot compare such love. I only know I have both, and they cannot be separated." He appealed to Nehemiah. "You understand, my uncle, do you not?"

"Of course, my child." Nehemiah's eyes were wet. "How could I not?"

"I'm not so sure I do." Oebazus said. "But why should I argue? A great many years lie ahead of you before you will have to decide. I imagine you will change your mind a dozen times, Bani."

Bani smiled sadly. And so too did Nehemiah. But neither said a word. They knew.

Covenant Books

Stories of Jewish Men and Women To Inspire and Instruct Young People